"Perhaps when you're back in England?" Dark brows rose hopefully.

"Not now, not ever," she told him, furious both with him for kissing her and herself for being so weak. "This is the one and only time I shall ever let you touch me. Call it a mental aberration, a moment of madness, or whatever you like—but it won't happen again."

"You sound very sure about that."

Born in the industrial heart of England, **MARGARET MAYO** now lives in a Staffordshire countryside village. She became a writer by accident, after attempting to write a short story when she was almost forty, and now writing is one of the most enjoyable parts of her life. She combines her hobby of photography with her research.

Dangerous Game

MARGARET MAYO

SWEET REVENGE

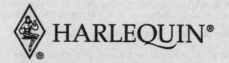

HARLEQUIN®

TORONTO • NEW YORK • LONDON
AMSTERDAM • PARIS • SYDNEY • HAMBURG
STOCKHOLM • ATHENS • TOKYO • MILAN • MADRID
PRAGUE • WARSAW • BUDAPEST • AUCKLAND

ISBN 0-373-80545-4

DANGEROUS GAME

First North American Publication 2001.

Copyright © 1999 by Margaret Mayo.

Visit us at www.eHarlequin.com

Printed in U.S.A.

CHAPTER ONE

'YOU do realise,' said Adam Sterne, 'that this is a full-time job, and when I say full-time I mean twenty-four hours a day. Is that understood?' His thickly fringed rich brown eyes were narrowed, his hard face unsmiling.

Penny nodded. 'I understand perfectly.'

'You don't mind that you'll have no time for yourself?'

She returned his gaze steadily. He was a handsome man, with a good strong jawline, an angular, chiselled face, and an incredibly sensual mouth. It was strange she hadn't noticed anything sensual about him before.

Her memories were of a cruel, ruthless tyrant, a hard-faced man, a man who never considered other people's feelings. 'I expected that when I applied for the job, Mr Sterne,' she told him firmly. 'It's no hardship.'

'Good.' He appraised her thoroughly for a further few seconds. 'Actually, I find it difficult to accept that such an attractive woman should want to commit herself to something like this for the next three months.'

Attractive woman! She should have been flattered but she wasn't; she barely even heard the compliment. 'I wouldn't have applied for the job if I hadn't been willing to give up my spare time,' she told him with a faint smile, a difficult smile. She had no reason to smile where this man was concerned. 'It's not as though it's for ever.'

'Are you suffering from a broken heart? Have you been let down by a man? Is that it?' As he spoke he pushed himself up and, skirting his desk, strode over to her, a tall,

lithe man in his late thirties, strong, dominating, powerful—
and totally, totally male.

'Something like that.' Her lips twisted wryly. He really
had no idea, none at all. 'I have no wish to discuss it.'

He continued to look at her, thoughtfully and speculatively. 'Have we met before, Miss Brooklyn?'

Penny froze. The last thing she wanted was for him to
recognise her. She stood up also, and faced him boldly,
almost daring him to say it again. She was five-nine in her
stockinged feet and her heels made her almost as tall as he
was. Sometimes she hated her height, but on this occasion
it was a definite advantage.

'I'm sure I would remember if we had,' she said pleasantly. 'You're not the sort of man a woman would easily
forget.' She even allowed a touch of huskiness in her tone.

Then from sheer force of habit she tossed her shoulder-
length mousy brown hair back from her face, before realising that it wasn't there, remembering that she had had it
cut dramatically short and dyed to an attractive honey-
blonde.

'And you're a very striking woman,' he returned, fingers
brushing his chin thoughtfully.

'I don't think looks have anything to do with the job,'
said Penny, striving desperately to keep calm. She mustn't
ruin the interview now.

To her relief he nodded. 'You're right, though I wouldn't
wish to impose upon my mother someone who wasn't
pleasant to look at.'

'Of course not.'

'And naturally temperament is vitally important. My
mother is a very irascible, querulous lady, impossible at
times. Do you think you can handle her?'

He looked at her doubtfully as he spoke, but Penny
firmed her shoulders and looked him straight in the eye. 'I

don't foresee any problem,' she replied evenly. 'But I would prefer to see your mother first—if I'm offered the job. And I'm sure she'll want to see for herself who her companion is going to be. Why isn't she conducting the interviews?'

'It's too tiring for her,' he answered brusquely. 'Besides, it was my idea that she have a companion on this holiday, so the decision will be mine. But, yes, I'll take you to see her.'

Penny's huge green eyes widened in surprise. 'You mean I have the job?' She hid her elation. The interview had gone better than she'd expected, much, much better—just that one hitch when he'd asked whether they'd met before. If only he knew!

With a bit luck—or maybe a lot—he would never associate the dowdy, timid Alex Brooke who had once worked for Sterne Securities with the ultra-smart and confident Penny Brooklyn now standing before him—at least not until she wanted him to know.

It was not as though she was actually lying, just twisting the truth—Penny was her middle name, and she'd simply tagged on her mother's Christian name to Brooke.

He nodded now. 'So long as my mother approves of you, then, yes, you have the job. I'm heartily fed up with interviewing unsuitable people. I'll need to check your references, of course, but—'

'Of course, Mr Sterne,' she said demurely. He would find nothing wrong with them; she'd made sure of that. All she'd needed was character references, and a couple of friends had willingly complied.

'Then we will go to my mother now.'

To Penny's dismay he took her elbow as he guided her through endless corridors. She wanted to snatch away, put space between them. She didn't want him to touch her—

and was alarmed at the tingle which shot through her veins, the surge of heat across her skin, sensations that were totally opposite to everything she felt for this man.

From the outside she had viewed his magnificent eighteenth-century house set in its acres of well-kept grounds with contempt, and she didn't change her mind now.

It was a beautiful place, the perfect background for a wealthy man, but she guessed it was for show only. This man was uncaring and unfeeling about anyone or anything except perhaps his mother. He really did seem to care for her. It was a surprising discovery. But he wouldn't appreciate the fine architecture or the glorious pieces of furniture glowing warmly with the patina of age.

Penny instinctively wanted to pause, to stroke her fingers across the wood, to feel, to appreciate, but his hand on her arm urged her forward.

'Nearly there now,' he said as they turned a final corner. 'My mother is well and truly tucked away, as you can see, but she likes it this way. She rarely leaves her rooms these days, and it will probably be like this on her holiday—and naturally you'll stay with her. She's not as independent as she likes to think. I should hate anything to happen to her because you're having a ball somewhere else.'

The threat in his voice angered Penny, made her want to strike out. This was how she remembered him. This was his callous, dominant side, the uncaring side, that gave no consideration for people's feelings, and it took all her self-control to sound calm and reasonable. 'Of course, Mr Sterne. I completely understand what's expected of me. I shall not let you down.'

He glanced at her, a frown tugging his dark brows together. Clearly she hadn't quite managed to hide her stormy feelings. But when he spoke again it was to say, 'Your family doesn't mind that you'll be away for three months?'

'My mother's dead,' she answered abruptly. 'She had a heart condition and it didn't stand up to some bad news a few months ago.'

'I'm sorry,' he said. 'And your father?'

'I don't remember him. He died when I was two.'

'And you say you have no brothers or sisters?'

'That's right,' she answered crisply. She had told him all this earlier. Why was he bringing it up again?

'And no boyfriend?'

Penny gritted her teeth as she shook her head. 'I'm all alone.' *Thanks to you!* 'You need have no fears that some-one will lay claim to my time.'

'That's good.'

He let go her arm at last, although she could still feel the pressure of his fingers, and she rubbed at the spot un-consciously, as though trying to wipe away his touch. He tapped on the panelled oak door facing them, then turned the knob and stepped inside before standing back for her to enter.

She could immediately see why his mother had chosen to live in this corner of the house. The room was light and airy, with windows on two sides, and was bathed in morn-ing sunshine—admittedly winter sun, with little warmth, but nevertheless it cheered the room, and the elderly lady who looked expectantly at them was nothing like the frail person Adam Sterne had depicted.

In fact when she stood up and came to greet them she looked as strong as an ox—despite the fact that she used a walking stick. She was tall, like her son, very upright, very slim, with thin features and blue button eyes that gave Penny the swift once-over.

'So this is your latest contestant, Adam, dear?'

She made it sound as though he was playing some sort of game, thought Penny, but she was determined not to be put down. This job was too important. So instead of waiting for Adam to answer she reached out her hand. 'I'm Penny Brooklyn,' she said pleasantly. 'Your son's offered me the job of companion on your holiday—so long as we *both* approve, of course.'

It was her emphasis on the word 'both' that caused Lucy Sterne's thin grey eyebrows to rise. Quite clearly she was not used to people being so forthright.

'Indeed,' the woman said.

Her hand was cool, despite the central heating and the log fire burning brightly in the grate, her ringless fingers swollen and bent with arthritis, and close up Penny could see lines of pain on her face and in the watery blue of her eyes. Nevertheless Lucy Sterne looked a proud woman, who would never admit to any illness or discomfort. Maybe being her companion would not be quite the trial Adam had suggested.

'Miss Brooklyn has no ties,' he informed his mother, 'and she's not in employment at the moment. So travelling with you next week won't be a problem.'

'Why aren't you working?' The question was thrust sharply, suspiciously.

Like mother like son, thought Penny. The same aggressive attitude, the same arrogant way of speaking to people they employed—or were about to employ. She had sudden doubts as to whether she was doing the right thing.

'I was made redundant from my last job,' she confessed, almost adding, *with a little help from your son*, before realising that this would do her no good at all. The whole point of changing her identity was so that he would not recognise her.

'Which was?'

'I was in design.' She was deliberately vague.

'So you haven't been a companion before?'

'No,' Penny admitted. 'But I don't see that there are any skills involved other than being good with people.'

'And are you?'

'I like to think so, and I did once train as a nurse.' Which was the truth, even though she'd never finished the course.

'But you didn't take it up as a career? Don't you think that was a waste of taxpayers' money?' asked Lucy Sterne accusingly.

Penny looked suitably penitent. 'It's something that has always troubled me.'

'And so it should,' retorted the older woman. 'But I appreciate your honesty, and if Adam approves then so do I. I was beginning to despair, to think that no one suitable existed on the face of the earth. And I think Adam was dreading the thought that he might have to come with me. The dear boy would hate that. He thinks his business interests cannot survive without him.' But she smiled at her son as she spoke, softening the words. 'I will, of course, need a great deal of your time. You do know that?'

Penny inclined her head. 'Your son has told me.'

'And you don't mind? You won't be looking for more entertaining company?'

'No, Mrs Sterne. I'll be quite content spending my days with you.'

The woman nodded. 'Good. That's good. I expect Adam has told you that it's doctor's orders I'm spending three months in the sun? This damned arthritis plays me up so in the English winters. I used to go away with Edward, every year without fail.'

'My father died three years ago and Mother hasn't been away since,' Adam explained.

'It won't be the same,' grumbled his parent.

'Nevertheless I'll do my best to see that you enjoy yourself,' said Penny.

It was exactly the right thing to say. The woman beamed, even Adam looked pleased, and when later he walked her out to her car he shook her hand warmly. 'I'm glad my mother likes you; I shall rest easy now. And to save you driving here on Tuesday I'll pick you up. Shall we say six-thirty?'

He was being very kind, thought Penny as she slid into her car—uncharacteristically so. And then his tone changed and he whipped out the order, 'Make sure you're ready.'

Penny almost saluted. Yes, sir. I'll be ready, sir. But instead she merely inclined her head, and without looking at him again she engaged gear and shot off at high speed.

Adam stood and watched until Penny's car disappeared from view. He still had the oddest feeling that he'd seen her somewhere before, although he felt quite sure that if he had he would never have forgotten her.

He liked tall women, especially when they weren't afraid of their height, when they held themselves tall and didn't resort to flat shoes. Penny Brooklyn was striking. Maybe her hair was a little too short, but it was beautifully styled—in fact everything about her appealed to him. She was elegant, she was confident, she was all he liked in a woman.

Maybe it *wasn't* that he'd met her before but that she was the quintessential woman—the one he had been unconsciously seeking all his life. His mother despaired of him ever getting married, and at thirty-eight he could understand her feelings. There had been women in his life, of course, but none with whom he'd wanted to settle down. None had come up to his expectations.

He went to his mother now. 'Well, what do you think?' A smile softened the often harsh angles of his face, made him look much younger.

'I think she'll be more than adequate,' returned the older

woman. 'You've done well, Adam. What are *your* feelings for her?'

His mother was direct, as always, and Adam half suspected that she'd already guessed he was more than a little interested. 'She'll be perfect for you, Mother. No ties, nothing to whisk her back to England at an inopportune moment. It's lucky we found her.'

'Do you find her attractive?'

'Mother!' He tried to sound scandalised. 'I simply looked at her as a potential companion for you.'

'You didn't see how beautiful she is? How stylish? Exactly the sort of woman I'd choose as—'

'Mother!'

'I'm sorry, Adam, but it really is time you found yourself a wife. Do you realise that I'm almost eighty and have no grandchildren?'

'As you were thirty-nine when you got married you have no room to talk, Mother dear,' he said quietly and firmly. 'Shall I ask Isabel to bring in lunch?'

'I'm not hungry,' she retorted.

'Not even if I stay and have it with you?'

The woman's thin brows rose. 'You're not rushing straight back to work?'

Adam smiled indulgently. 'It can wait another couple of hours.' And if his mother wanted to talk about Penny Brooklyn he wouldn't stop her. In fact he'd like that very much indeed!

Penny snapped the locks on her suitcase. She was ready. Time now to sit down and enjoy a cup of coffee before Adam Sterne arrived.

She'd spent the last few days getting used to the idea that she was going to work for his mother. Hopefully she'd find out all about him, find some way to pay him back for the grief and unhappiness he'd caused her, the pain and humiliation.

Well before half past six the doorbell pealed impatiently. Penny jumped to her feet, and in so doing spilled her coffee down her brand-new white cotton trousers. Furious with both herself and Adam Sterne, she scowled at him as she opened the door. 'One short ring would have done.'

Adam smiled, unperturbed. 'I thought you might have overslept.'

He wore a black polo-necked shirt under a dark grey suit, and maybe if she hadn't known him for what he was she would have thought him mysterious and exciting. Instead he looked menacing, and she scowled again. 'Well, I didn't, and I was ready—and now I've got to change because you made me spill my damned coffee.'

'*I* did?' Well-shaped dark brows rose in a marked question.

'If you hadn't kept your finger on the bell I wouldn't have got up quite so quickly. I suppose you'd better come in.'

She hadn't planned on asking him in, hadn't wanted him to compare her own tiny, cramped home to his palatial mansion. She'd lived her whole life with her mother in this terraced house in Thwaite in North Yorkshire and was perfectly content.

The main door opened into what her mother had simply called the front room, a room that was used only when visitors came. Beyond that was a cosy living room, with red velvet curtains and a red floral three-piece suite, and at the back of the house was the kitchen. Upstairs one of the original three bedrooms had been turned into a reasonably spacious bathroom.

'It's not much but it's mine and I like it,' she declared

defensively as she led him through to her living room and saw that he was taking everything in.

'I can see why,' he said with a warm smile. 'It's cosy, very cosy indeed.'

She had been so sure he would say something derogatory that she looked at him in astonishment. 'You think so?'

'I do,' he admitted. 'I rattle around Whitestone Manor like a lost soul. But it's my mother's family house and she adores it. I moved back in when my father died and I wouldn't dream of leaving while she's still alive. You look surprised.'

'I am,' Penny admitted. 'It struck me as being your sort of place, the perfect residence for someone like you.'

A swift questioning frown daggered his brows, narrowed those expressive dark eyes. 'What do you mean, someone like me?'

The wrong thing to have said! He wasn't to know that she already knew exactly who he was. But in for a penny in for a pound. She lifted her shoulders and tried to look casual. 'From what your mother said I assume you're a successful businessman, so I simply thought Whitestone Manor was ideal for corporate entertaining, that's all.' She really would have to be careful what she said. At this stage it was crucial that she remain on good terms with him.

His face relaxed, lost it suspiciousness. 'Mmm, yes, I see how you could have deduced that, but I don't like people making assumptions about me. I'd prefer you kept your thoughts to yourself. Is that clear?'

'Perfectly clear,' she answered pleasantly. 'I apologise for speaking out of turn. Please, sit down while I nip upstairs and change.'

She was cross about the trousers, as she'd bought them especially for the flight. She sluiced the coffee stain with cold water and hung them over the bath to dry before pulling on another pair. Her neighbour was keeping an eye on the house and would hopefully tidy them away when they were dry.

Downstairs, Adam was looking at a photograph of her mother on the mantelpiece. 'You look like her. Was she tall also?'

Penny shook her head. 'Quite tiny, as a matter of fact. I apparently take after my father. Shall we go?' She didn't like the idea that he'd been nosying around the room in her absence.

He picked up her suitcase. 'Is this all?'

Penny nodded.

'For three months?'

'I can't see that I'll need much if most of my time is spent indoors with your mother. In any case it's nearly all drip-dry.'

His lips turned down at the corners. 'I'm impressed. Most women I know would take a trunkload. But if you do find yourself short of anything then I'll naturally foot the bill.'

'That's very generous of you.' Considering generosity was not one of his strong points. In fact she would say it was one of his weaknesses. He certainly hadn't been generous where *she* was concerned.

Once seated in his black BMW, Penny found to her dismay that it was impossible to dismiss him. She felt an awareness that was unbelievable, given the circumstances.

Her eyes were drawn to long legs stretched out, to thigh muscles bulging beneath fine wool, to long-fingered hands lightly holding the wheel—hands that had touched her arm and sent flames of fire licking through her veins, hands which it was easy to imagine caressing her breasts.

Her nipples hardened at the unexpected, unwanted thought—Lord knew where it had come from. She almost gasped at the audacity of it, and determinedly turned to stare out of the window, to ignore him, to pretend he wasn't there.

It was impossible. His aftershave, which she recognised as a favourite of hers, was an aphrodisiac in itself. Goodness, what was happening to make her feel this way? She ought not to entertain even the faintest of emotions, certainly not this rip-roaring blood through her veins, the quickening of her senses.

'Is something wrong?'

Penny remained hunched where she was, fingernails digging painfully into palms, her eyes blank and staring straight ahead. 'Why should there be?'

'It's as though you're trying to shut me out.'

'I can't think why I'd want to do that.' With an effort she faced him, forced a smile, jammed her traitorous feelings into a dark corner of her mind. Why hadn't he sent a car for her instead of coming himself? Why was he torturing her so?

Except of course he didn't know who she was—had no idea. And if he ever found out he would dismiss her out of his life—and his mother's—as swiftly, as dispassionately, as callously, as he had done once before.

'Are you worried about what's in store?' There was real concern in the deep, sexy tones of his voice, compassion in the velvet darkness of his eyes.

Every muscle in Penny's body tightened. 'I—I guess I'm a little nervous.' But not of the job, *of him*! Of her reaction to him. It was damning. It was unbelievable. It was cruel. It was making a mockery of all that had gone before.

He smiled, a warm, all-encompassing smile that sent fresh rivers of warmth through her veins. 'You have no need to be,' he said softly. 'My mother's done nothing but talk warmly about you. She thinks you'll be the perfect companion. She's congratulated me over and over again on finding you. I have only one request—that you don't let her down.'

In Penny's confused state it didn't sound like a request; it sounded like an order. She tossed her head, clear green eyes flashing. 'You don't have to tell me again, Mr Sterne. You made it *very* clear at my interview; I haven't forgotten.'

'Something tells me you don't like me, Miss Brooklyn.' His eyes penetrated hers for a brief second. 'Or am I imagining it?'

Penny swallowed hard. She wasn't handling this well. It was important to keep him on side—for the time being. She forced another smile. 'I'm sorry if you got that impression. It wasn't intentional. I'm just not very good first thing in the morning.'

'Especially when someone makes you spill coffee down your trousers?' he asked wryly. 'If it will make you feel any better I humbly apologise.'

The great Adam Sterne, apologising? The man who cared not a jot for other people's feelings—only that Sterne Securities ran faultlessly and made him heaps of money?

It was a relief when he drew the car to a halt outside Whitestone Manor. Penny climbed out quickly and followed him indoors. His mother was ready and waiting, as was a trio of matching suitcases and other assorted luggage. 'Good, you're here,' she said. 'I was afraid you might change your mind.'

'I'm looking forward to it,' said Penny with the warmest of smiles.

'No second thoughts about tying yourself to an old lady for three months?'

'None at all,' said Penny, still smiling.

Lucy Sterne nodded her satisfaction. 'You did well, Adam,' she acclaimed.

Glancing at him, Penny saw that he was looking at her with a frown of fierce concentration. It was gone immediately, replaced by a nod and a smile, but she guessed he'd been wondering why she was so distant with him and yet warm and friendly towards his mother.

She turned away. 'Can I help you with anything, Mrs Sterne?'

In the car to the airport Lucy Sterne took the back seat, insisting that Penny sit beside her son. 'Your duties haven't yet begun,' she told her with a dry smile.

Penny slumped back and closed her eyes. It was the only way she could shut Adam out—but instead her thoughts went back to the other time they had met, the one and only time, to the occasion when he had damned her to hell...

CHAPTER TWO

'MR STERNE wants to see you, Alex.'

Alex looked at Donna in real concern. 'But why? I didn't do it. I swear I didn't.'

'Tell him that. If you're innocent you have nothing to worry about.' Donna Jackson, senior designer, was for some reason always hostile towards Alex. Even now there was no smile of comfort on her carefully made up face, almost a glitter of malice in her blue eyes, although Alex was far too upset to see it.

The trouble was no one in the office believed that Alex was not guilty. Never in the whole history of Sterne Securities had anyone ever leaked information to their competitors. And as Alex had been the last to join the company the blame lay with her. Her pleas of innocence had gone ignored.

And now the head of the company wanted to see her.

She was well aware of the fact that he was a hard man to please, that he had a reputation for coming down on his employees like a ton of hot bricks if they didn't do their jobs properly. She wasn't the first person to have been summoned before him, and there were tales of people leaving his office in tears. On the other hand he was quick to praise if work was done well and he paid exceedingly high wages—which was one of the reasons people rarely left his employ.

Jonathon Byrne, her fiancé, had got her the job. He'd worked for Adam Sterne ever since graduating from university, and quickly made his way up to technical director.

When Sterne Securities had been in the process of expanding their design department he'd persuaded her to apply for a job. 'It will be much better wages than you're getting now,' he'd told her, 'And they're a great crowd to work with.'

Now, even Jonathon had his doubts about her innocence. They had talked about it last night over supper, and although he'd said that he wanted to believe her, he didn't see how it could have been anyone else.

'Everyone's been with Sterne for years,' he pointed out. 'We've never had this sort of problem before. I know you might not have intended to let slip what you were working on, but—'

'*I didn't,*' Alex quickly asserted. 'How can you say that? I never mentioned it to anyone.'

'Alex, I want to believe you. You know I do. But it all points to you. This device stood to make Sterne hundreds of thousands, if not millions of pounds. Now it's all going to Sachs. And they're claiming the invention was their own.'

Jonathon, tall, good-looking, with gold-rimmed spectacles and a neat beard to disguise his youthful appearance, continued to look at her disapprovingly.

'I thought you of all people would believe me,' she said, disappointment choking her voice.

'I'm sorry, Alex, but I can't disregard the facts, however much I'd like to. I think it's time I went. I'll see you at work tomorrow.'

He had left without kissing her, the first time he'd ever done that, and Alex had felt utter despair. If Jonathon didn't believe her then what chance was there that anyone else would?

Now, as she made her way to Adam Sterne's inner sanctum on the top floor—a suite of rooms that no one went to unless they were invited—she felt tension build up inside her. It wasn't fair. Why would no one listen? It had to be someone else, someone who was letting her take the blame. But who? She didn't know. There was just no one who would do that sort of thing.

She tapped nervously on Adam Sterne's door, twisting her long medium-brown hair as she waited. As usual she had fixed it in a slide for neatness, and at this moment it hung forward over one hunched shoulder. With no make-up she looked pale and plain, and less than her twenty-six years, and with the flat shoes she always wore because she hated being so tall she knew that she looked clumsy and inelegant. Had she known that she was going to be summoned here today...

'Come.'

Adam Sterne's loud, peremptory voice made her more nervous than ever, and she opened the door fearfully, then closed it silently behind her. She had only ever caught glimpses of him as he strode through his empire, never spoken to him before, and as she stood inside the room looking at him she wondered why she was feeling so apprehensive. She was almost acting as though she was guilty, dammit.

She straightened her back and moved slowly across the carpeted room. It was a big room, a luxurious room, with fine oak furniture and deep leather chairs, and banks of glossy green plants which relieved the plainness of the walls and carpet.

'Sit,' the voice commanded.

He made her sound like a dog, thought Alex, but she obeyed—before her legs gave way. They felt as though they were stuffed with cotton wool instead of muscle and bone. He was the most intimidating man she had ever met, and it was immediately apparent that all was not going to go well.

His expression was merciless as he looked at her across his massive desk, hands splayed in front of him—big hands, with well-manicured nails, she thought inconsequentially—brown eyes glittering with the cold hardness of polished stone, dark hair brushed severely back.

'Never,' he said, the tone of his voice matching the harshness of his face, 'in the whole history of this company, has anyone *ever* let me down, sold me down the river the way you have.'

'But I didn't,' said Alex, trying to inject confidence into her voice. But in the face of such damning hostility it came out like a squeak, making her sound guilty even though she wasn't. She cleared her throat and began again. 'If you would—'

But he gave her no chance to speak. 'I expect my employees to have integrity. I do not expect them to line their own pockets by—'

'But, Mr Sterne, I did not—'

'*Silence!* I know exactly what you've done, and you can rest assured, Miss Alexandra Brooke, that I shall take this matter to its ultimate end. No one—I repeat, *no one*—crosses me and gets away with it.' His dark, condemning eyes stabbed through her with such ferocity that she almost felt a physical pain. 'Regardless of the outcome of the court case, your employment with this company is terminated as from now.'

'You're taking me to court?' It was little more than a breathless whisper. She had not expected this. To lose her job maybe, almost certainly, but to be officially charged with committing the crime—it wasn't possible. He couldn't do this. She was innocent.

'You can bet I am.'

'Without even listening to my side of the story?' That was why she had thought she was here, to tell her tale. No one else had wanted to hear it. They all had her hung, drawn and quartered without a hearing.

'What is there to listen to?' he demanded of her now. 'It's as clear to me as the nose on your face that you're guilty. *If* you're not, and I say *if* reservedly, then it will be up to the judge and jury to find out. I do not intend wasting any more of my time with you.' His dark eyes still glared accusingly and damningly into hers. 'Good day.'

Alex couldn't move. She sat there and looked at him, at this monster who was not giving her a chance. 'You can't do this to me,' she said, every ounce of colour draining from her face. Even her lips were bloodless, and breathing was almost impossible. It was as though someone had punched her in the stomach and knocked every breath of air out of her.

'Oh, believe me, I can, and I am,' he retorted coldly, rising to his feet as he spoke. 'There is nothing you can say that will make me change my mind. Not a thing. What you did is nothing short of industrial espionage—and I'm sure you know what the consequences of that are without me telling you.'

He was tall, six three or four at a guess, and he held himself arrogantly proud as he marched to the door and yanked it open. He was giving Alex no choice. As far as he was concerned it was over; she was guilty and that was that.

She pushed herself up and made her way back across the room with legs as heavy as lead. It took for ever to reach his side. He stood stiffly erect and didn't look at her. Alex felt like spitting in his face, but of course she didn't. She did have integrity, despite his thoughts to the contrary.

'Thanks for nothing, Mr Sterne.' She held herself upright

too, so that her eyes were almost, but not quite, on a level with his, her tone icy. 'I hope that if ever you're in trouble you don't have to put yourself in the hands of someone as implacable as you. I hope someone will have the decency to listen to your side of the story.'

He didn't answer, and she heard the door close with a resolute thud behind her.

'Wake up, Miss Brooklyn.'

The well-remembered voice penetrated her thoughts, shot open her eyes, added fuel to the fire burning in her stomach.

Adam Sterne saw the hostility on her face and frowned. 'Is something wrong?'

Penny pulled herself quickly together as she realised that they had reached the airport. It wouldn't do for him to have a clue at this stage to what she was planning. 'I'm sorry, I was dreaming.'

'And not a happy dream by the look of things?'

If he was probing she had no intention of answering. She gave a faint smile and shook her head.

They were taken to the VIP lounge, Adam dealing briskly and efficiently with the formalities, and it seemed no time at all before they were being asked to board their aircraft.

Penny's relief at saying goodbye to Adam Sterne was faint. Even though there would be thousands of miles between them he would never be out of her mind. She'd planned this job to find out more about him, to try and discover his Achilles' heel, but now she was not so sure that it was a good idea. She hadn't expected to feel a sexual awareness of him, an ignition of her body that could prove her downfall.

Even shaking his hand sent an ocean of currents crashing

through her, and it was all she could do to smile and re-
assure him that she would take every care of his mother.

'I'll obviously be in touch from time to time,' he told
her, his tone deadly serious.

'And I will contact you if anything should go wrong,'
she returned.

'Make sure that you do,' he said firmly. 'Don't let my
mother extract any promises to keep things from me. I'm
holding you entirely responsible.'

Penny frowned. 'Are you anticipating problems?' She
wished he would let go her hand. Why was he still holding
it? Why was he looking so intently into her face?

'Not at all, but I believe in being prepared.'

'In that case, Mr Sterne,' she said solemnly, 'I will phone
you if your mother so much as sneezes.'

He smiled then. 'I don't think you need take things quite
that far, Miss Brooklyn—Penny. I may call you that?'

She inclined her head. 'If you wish.'

'And you must call me Adam.'

'Oh, no,' she said quickly, perhaps too quickly, because
he frowned. 'That wouldn't be right.' It would bring him
much closer and that was the last thing she wanted. There
could be no intimacy between them whatsoever if her plan
was to work.

'Right?' he asked. 'Why wouldn't it be right?'

'You're my employer.'

Thick brows rose with a touch of impatience. 'We're not
living in the Dark Ages.' And then, on a softer, more con-
ciliatory note, 'Adam it is, Penny. I'm almost sorry I'm not
coming with you.'

She lifted her brows, ignoring her triggered heartbeats at
the thought of sharing a holiday with this blatantly sexy
man. 'If you accompanied your mother there would be no
need for me.'

'True,' he agreed, 'but I think it would be a pleasurable experience.'

Penny frowned. 'What do you mean?'

'You and me.'

'Me and you—a pleasurable experience?' Penny swallowed her unease and managed to sound incredulous. 'I'm being employed as your mother's companion and nothing more. If you remember, you made a point of telling me that this was a business arrangement.'

'Indeed I did,' he said with a smile. 'And unfortunately it's business that will keep me away. But maybe when this holiday's over...'

Penny shook her head. 'You're confusing me.'

'Am I? I don't think you can deny that there's a certain mutual attraction.'

His hand tightened on hers until she felt he might crush her slender bones, and the velvety darkness of his eyes slowly traced every inch of her face.

'Mutual attraction, Mr Sterne?' She injected horror into her voice. 'You must be imagining things.' Lord, was she really hearing this?

'Oh, I don't think so.' A faint smile lifted the corners of his mouth. 'I think the reason you're cool and distant towards me is to hide your real feelings. And very commendable, too. I've had my fair share of women who openly show an interest in me. It's refreshingly different to find someone so—restrained.'

'You have a vivid imagination, Mr Sterne—Adam,' she retorted fiercely. 'I am not, nor ever will be, attracted to you. Nor is this the time for such a conversation. Your mother is waiting.'

The fact that he knew his touch affected her made everything worse. This was humiliating. Had she really given herself away? Of only one thing could she be thankful—

he hadn't recognised her as the woman he'd dismissed so damningly from his company.

It was small consolation.

As they boarded the plane it was a relief to leave him behind. If he had gone on much longer in the same vein she wouldn't have been able to keep her feelings hidden. It was sheer madness that she felt anything for him—and if she allowed her feelings free reign it would be a death blow to her plans.

First class was impressive. The only way to travel, she thought—if money was no object. She and Lucy talked for a while, but it wasn't long before Adam's mother declared that she was tired.

Immediately a stewardess reclined her seat and tucked a blanket around her. 'Don't let anyone wake me,' Lucy admonished. 'Not until we get there.'

Penny tried to concentrate on the morning newspaper. It was impossible. Adam Sterne's handsome face swam before her eyes and no matter how she tried she couldn't dismiss him from her thoughts.

In the end she put the paper down and closed her eyes also. If she couldn't forget him then she might as well indulge in thinking about him. But not thoughts of mutual attraction. She needed to fuel her fire, bank it up as high as she dared; she needed to forcefully remind herself that he was her arch enemy.

Easier said than done. All she could remember were the sparks of ignition when his hand touched hers, the flames of fire when his deep brown eyes made their slow appraisal. It was immoral that these thoughts should take precedence, and an even worse state of affairs that she could do nothing about it.

She was seeing him now as one highly sexy man. She was seeing a side that she'd never seen before, never expected to see, didn't want to see! He had ruined her life and she had convinced herself she hated him. Why, then, this—and she hated to admit it—this physical attraction?

He was right, damn him, she *was* attracted, but it had shocked her to hear that he too was attracted to her. Had he meant it? Or was he playing games? Trying to find out what sort of person she was? What he could get away with? How far she would let him go?

She didn't realise that her breathing had noticeably deepened until Lucy Sterne said, 'Are you all right, Penny, my dear?'

Turning her head, she saw that Adam's mother was watching her, a faint frown on her brow. 'Are you afraid of flying?'

Penny shook her head. 'It's nothing, Mrs Sterne. I was just thinking about something unpleasant.' Fingers crossed that she didn't ask what it was.

'I see. I was beginning to feel worried about you.'

With an effort Penny smiled. She really would have to be careful. 'Please, it was nothing. I'm sorry. I'm the one who should be worrying about you.'

'I hope my son hasn't been filling your head with lots of nonsense about my health?' Lucy Sterne said waspishly. 'I don't need you to keep a constant eye on me. I hate people who hover, who try to anticipate my every need. And Adam knows that. Rest assured I shall let you know when I want you to do anything.'

'I'll remember.' Penny smiled warmly at the older woman, who nodded, satisfied, then closed her eyes again and slept for the rest of the flight.

As they neared St Lucia, as the lush green island sitting in a perfect blue sea got bigger and bigger, Penny began at last to feel excited. A three-month holiday in the Caribbean was beyond her wildest dreams, and the thought of swimming in clear warm waters, of sunbathing on powder-white sands, of totally relaxing with nothing to do except keep her eye on Lucy Sterne, was like balm to her ruffled nerves.

She would be able to forget the trauma of being wrongly accused of something she hadn't done, the hardship she had subsequently suffered, and concentrate on enjoying a completely different and luxurious lifestyle.

'You'll like Adam's villa,' said Mrs Sterne as the plane began its final descent.

'It belongs to your son?' Penny frowned. He hadn't given that impression.

Lucy smiled. 'Yes. He bought it when his business began to take off so that his father and I could use it. He's a wonderful son, Penny. So thoughtful, so kind and caring, I couldn't wish for anyone better.'

Kind? Caring? Adam? Did his mother really know him? Did she know the true Adam, or only the side that he wished her to see? Penny would have loved to tell her about the way she'd been treated, but knew she didn't dare. It was doubtful whether the woman would believe her anyway. As far as Lucy Sterne was concerned the sun shone out of her offspring's eyes.

'He never uses it himself,' Lucy went on. 'The last three years a friend of his has rented it, but it's empty again now, and I can't tell you how much I'm looking forward to this holiday. It will be strange, admittedly, without Edward— so many memories.' Her pale blue eyes were for a moment sadly retrospective. 'But with you to cheer me I'm sure we'll both enjoy it.'

'I'm looking forward to it too, Mrs Sterne,' said Penny sincerely. Although there was a hidden motive for her obtaining this job there was no denying it would be an enjoyable experience.

'Have you ever been to the Caribbean before?'

Penny shook her head. 'I'm afraid Spain is my limit. I could never afford anything as luxurious as this.'

'Then you're in for a real treat, my dear.'

They both looked out of the window as the ground rushed up to meet them, and when they finally stepped outside the heat was like a blast from a furnace.

Penny was afraid it might be too much for Adam's mother, but the woman was smiling. 'Isn't it wonderful?' she asked. 'The villa's air-conditioned, of course, but I love the heat. I can feel it warming my bones already.'

But she would soon wilt if she stayed in it for very long, thought Penny, and as soon as their luggage appeared she ushered her towards the line of waiting taxis.

'No, no,' said Mrs Sterne, 'I have my own driver. He'll be around somewhere. Ah, there he is. Fabian!' She waved her hand in the air.

Fabian's round black face lit with a smile. 'Welcome back, Mrs Sterne. It's good to see you again.'

'I'm pleased to be here,' she said. 'It's been far too long. Let me introduce Penny; she's come to keep me company. Penny, this is Fabian, who looks after the property.'

A small, rotund man with an eternal smile shook Penny's hand. 'Welcome to St Lucia, Miss Penny. Have you been here before?'

'Sadly, I haven't,' she answered.

'Then you must allow me to show you around our beautiful island—if Mrs Sterne permits?'

'You can take us both,' said the older woman warmly. 'In a few days' time, perhaps, when we've recovered from the flight.'

Penny, looking eagerly out of the window as they began their journey, was amazed to discover that they drove on the same side of the road as in England. But here the similarity ended.

It was as green as England, yes, but the vegetation was vastly different: bananas and mangoes were growing by the roadside, avocados, cashew nuts, papayas, and flame-red poinsettias as tall as a man. It was just incredible. So new and exciting that she couldn't take her eyes off it.

She spotted an iguana, sunning itself on the branch of a tree, and a couple of cows tethered at the edge of the road.

North of Castries, the capital, which was an extremely busy place, a lot of hotel and villa development had taken place. This was obviously where most people spent their holidays, thought Penny.

The Villa Mimosa was set in a good acre of ground, perched on a hillside overlooking the Atlantic. It was an absolutely delightful pink-painted building and Penny fell in love with it immediately.

It was a low, sprawling L-shaped property, with arches and sun decks and a pool, and plenty of trees to provide shade. A perfect retreat, and she could see why Lucy and Edward had loved coming here.

'Doesn't Adam *ever* use it?' she asked, still staring with wonder at this idyllic home.

'Never,' answered his mother shortly. 'He reckons he's always too busy to take holidays. He travels abroad, yes, but it's always on business. He has offshoots of his company all over the world. He rarely relaxes. It's no wonder he's never found himself a wife. No woman would put up with his hectic lifestyle.'

Inside, all was cool and light. There were three bedrooms, each with their own bathroom, and a dining and living area divided by an archway. Everything was white, with a profusion of pot plants and jade-green curtains and shutters.

The sunlight on the pool reflected moving shadows in the house, and Penny felt that it was like being in an underwater grotto. It was like nothing she had ever experienced, and far exceeded her expectations. This was another world; it was going to be sheer pleasure, and she might even forget the reason she had applied for the job.

Lucy Sterne sat in a deep armchair in her bedroom as Penny unpacked her clothes, her head back, her eyes closed. She looked tired, even though she'd slept most of the flight.

They'd been in the air for roughly nine hours, and with the time difference it meant that although it was only early afternoon their body clocks were telling them it was early evening.

'I wish Adam would take time off and join us,' grumbled his mother.

Penny grimaced. It looked as though she wasn't going to be allowed to forget him.

'You don't think it a good idea?'

'I'm sorry?'

'You pulled a face when I mentioned my son. Don't you like him?' Lucy looked at Penny in consternation, as though her answer was very important.

'I—er—of course.' What could she say? She had been unaware that the older woman was watching her. 'I hardly know him.'

'Maybe, but something tells me you have a grudge against him?'

This woman was astute, thought Penny, and saw far more than she'd given her credit for. She would have to watch herself carefully.

'Didn't he treat you well at the interview? He can be a bit brusque with people, a bit overpowering sometimes, but—'

'No, Mrs Sterne. All went well. I wasn't aware that I'd pulled a face; I must have been thinking of something else.'

'So you like Adam?'

Why was the woman insisting on pinning her down? And what did she say now? 'I really haven't had time to form an opinion,' she ventured, 'but if the way he looks after you is anything to go by then he has to be a very special person.'

Lucy Sterne relaxed and smiled. 'Indeed he is, and I'm sure that when you get to know him better you'll think so too.'

There was no chance of her getting to know him better, thought Penny, not a cat in hell's chance. Obviously his mother didn't know that he had a hard, ruthless side, didn't know that he could cut the ground from beneath your feet at a single slice.

They spent the rest of the day sitting around, being waited on by Maggie, Fabian's wife, who was cook and housekeeper and everything else rolled into one. Between them, these two good-natured St Lucians ran the whole place like clockwork. Penny felt redundant, couldn't see why she'd been asked to accompany Lucy Sterne when she had these loyal people looking after her.

She soon began to realise, however, that life was not easy with Lucy Sterne. If she wasn't asking Penny to read the newspaper to her, or find her sunglasses, or write some letters, she wanted her clothes pressed—and she didn't want Maggie to do it, she wanted Penny. She wanted to dress in something warmer—or cooler; she wanted a drink—no, not cold, hot; wanted to sit outside or come indoors. She never seemed satisfied for more than a few minutes at a time.

Adam had been right when he'd said that she would never have time for herself. His mother was constantly demanding—unfailingly polite, yes, but nevertheless she had Penny running round like a demented rabbit.

One afternoon Lucy Sterne woke from her usual after-lunch nap and said crossly, 'It's about time I heard from Adam. You'd better call him.'

Penny didn't tell her that she'd spoken to him only yesterday. Mrs Sterne's memory wasn't always as good as she liked to think it was, but Penny had found that it didn't pay to argue. It was with a rapidly beating heart, however, that she picked up the phone and dialled Adam's number.

Each time he'd phoned the Villa Mimosa Adam had hoped that Penny might answer—and each time it had been either Maggie or Fabian who'd picked up the phone.

It was the first time in his life that a woman had taken precedence over work, over his life in fact; he couldn't get Penny Brooklyn out of his mind. He went to bed thinking about her, fantasising about her, imagining her next to him, feeling the sweet-scented warmth of her body, touching her, holding her, making love to her.

When finally he slept he then dreamt about her, and woke up with her in his thoughts—and the fantasy started all over again. It was destroying his life—and other people were noticing it. Bill Bates, his senior sales executive and also an old friend, had asked whether he was ill. 'You've not been your usual self for days, Adam. I think you should take some time off. Perhaps you're overdoing it.'

Adam had scoffed at the idea, but actually taking time off and spending it with Penny Brooklyn was a very tantalising thought. Although exactly what it was about her that appealed to him he wasn't sure.

She was tall, and he liked that, she was stylish and sophisticated, which he appreciated, but there was also an air of mystery about her, as though she was hiding some deep, dark secret, and that intrigued him as well. Altogether she was a hell of an attractive woman, and the thought of waiting three months before he saw her again was driving him crazy.

Bill was right; he ought to take a holiday. Maybe he could join his mother and Penny in St Lucia? The thought excited him, sent his male hormones scudding. Should he do it, or shouldn't he? What would his mother think? He had rarely visited when she and his father had holidayed there. She would know it was because of Penny, and there'd be endless questions and sly comments and she would be for ever leaving the two of them alone together.

His hand hovered over the telephone. Should he or shouldn't he? Would it be wise or would he be making a fool of himself? It rang suddenly, and when he picked it up he knew that fate had stepped in and given him his answer.

'Mr Sterne—this is Penny Brooklyn.'

He smiled to himself. He had recognised her voice instantly, the softly hesitant tones triggering a tattoo within his breast, a surge in his groin. Oh, hell. How could one woman do this to him? A strange woman at that, someone he'd met only a couple of times.

He'd thought about her so much and now she was speaking to him, and if he closed his eyes he could imagine her in those slender-fitting white trousers she'd spilt the coffee down, and the lime sweater that had hidden none of her luscious curves. She'd blamed him for the coffee stain, and those green eyes, those beautiful green eyes, had flashed a thousand daggers. She had been incredibly beautiful in her anger.

'It's your mother. She's asked me to—'

'There's nothing wrong?' he cut in swiftly, guiltily. Lord, he should have been thinking about his parent, not Penny.

He should have acted the concerned son, not entertained highly erotic thoughts that played havoc with certain parts of his anatomy.

'No, no, she's fine.'

'Then what—?'

'Actually,' Penny cut in, 'she's complaining that you never phone her.'

'But I do, every day.'

'I know,' she said quietly, with a smile in her voice. 'But she forgets, and I didn't like to tell her because she would—'

'Snap your head off? I know, Penny.' He couldn't help smiling too. He was enjoying listening to her, talking to her, enjoying this brief moment of contact.

'I'll tell her you're on the line, Mr Sterne. I won't be a minute.'

'No, Penny, wait!' The words were out before he could stop them, making him feel slightly foolish. 'I'd like to speak with you first.'

There was silence at the other end as she waited to hear what he had to say. But how could he declare that he was missing her, thinking about her constantly, that he wanted to see her, to be with her, to hold her, to touch, to kiss, to…?

'Mr Sterne, are you still there?'

'It's Adam,' he reminded her. 'And, yes, I'm here. I just wanted to know how you are. Are you coping all right? My mother's not running you ragged?'

'Not yet,' she answered. 'I'm actually quite enjoying myself.'

'Excellent. I was—er—worried that you might find it all too much and decide to come home.'

'I wouldn't let your mother down,' she said at once, her voice sharp. 'Is that all you wanted to say?'

Not for the first time he had the feeling that she didn't like him, that she had no time for him. And yet there were other times when he could have sworn that she was attracted to him—as he was to her. Unless, of course, it was this she was fighting? The thought pleased him, brought the smile back to his face.

'For the time being,' he answered. But his mind was made up. He could keep away from her no longer.

CHAPTER THREE

IT TOOK Adam several days to rearrange his diary, and all the time he couldn't get Penny out of his thoughts. When finally he boarded the plane that would take him to her he had to deliver a stern lecture to himself to calm down. He hadn't felt like this since he was fifteen and had a crush on his maths teacher.

He'd not warned them of his visit, was looking forward to surprising his mother. She would be pleased, he knew, but it was difficult to gauge Penny's reaction.

She gave the impression of disliking him, and yet he'd felt the warmth rush through her at his touch, had seen the delicate colour in her cheeks.

He would tread carefully, treat her considerately, not rush into anything. And on such a beautiful island as St Lucia surely she couldn't fail to fall in love?

As the taxi drew to a halt in front of the Villa Mimosa Adam felt his heart beat that little bit faster, that little bit louder. It came as a crushing disappointment, therefore, to discover that his mother and Penny were not at home.

Maggie said, 'Fabian's taken them on a tour of the island. I'm not sure when they'll be back. Is your mother expecting you, Mr Sterne? Did she forget?'

'No, no, I thought I'd surprise her. It's my own fault. I'll take a swim—and I know it's a bit late but if there's any lunch going...?' He gave her one of his warmest smiles.

'Of course, Mr Sterne. I'll see to it at once.' Maggie, as thin and serious as her husband was round and cheerful, hurried away.

39

Adam slung his case on the bed, took out a pair of swimming trunks, and unleashed his frustration by doing several punishing lengths of the pool. It served him right; he shouldn't have got so excited. He shouldn't have built up his hopes so high.

He let the sun dry him off on one of the poolside loungers, and then ate his solitary lunch in the shade of the verandah which ran the full length of the house.

Afterwards he slept. He hadn't intended to, he'd planned to simply sit and watch and wait, wanting to see Penny before she saw him, but his eyes closed and the next thing he heard was his mother's voice.

'Adam!' It was an exclamation of pure pleasure.

He looked up and saw both his mother and Penny standing looking down at him. His parent was smiling happily, although disbelievingly, while Penny looked as if she'd seen a ghost. Without a doubt she was not at all pleased to see him.

'I can't believe you're here,' said his mother. 'What's happened?'

'I thought it time I took a holiday,' he answered, rising fluidly and giving his mother a bear hug.

'Why didn't you let me know? I would never have gone out. It's the first time since we've been here.' Her eyes were suspiciously moist. 'Fabian was anxious to show Penny the island, and I thought I'd go with them. Adam, this is wonderful. Are you staying long? I can't believe you're here. I've nagged you so often to take time off.'

'Then it looks as though your nagging's paid off,' he rejoined. 'But Bill Bates—you remember Bill?—he thought I needed a break as well, so here I am—and I've set no time limit on it.'

He let his mother go and turned to Penny. He wanted to hug her too, he wanted to kiss her and hold her for ever, but the barriers were up so instead he held out his hand. 'Hello, Penny.'

She looked gorgeous, even better than he remembered. Already her skin had been kissed by the sun, and her green sundress reflected the colour of her eyes. She was totally stunning—except for the fact that her lips were clamped tightly together, and the hand she reluctantly slipped into his was limp and without warmth.

'Mr Sterne,' she acknowledged quietly.

'How are you enjoying life on St Lucia?'

'It's very nice.'

'Nice,' snorted Lucy Sterne. 'She's been raving about the island all day, says it's the most beautiful place she's ever seen. I think you intimidate her, Adam. I think Penny's first impression of you was not a very good one.' She pointed a warning finger at him. 'I think you have a lot of making up to do.'

Adam wondered what Penny had been saying about him. He'd been a bit severe at the interview, admittedly, but he'd needed to make sure she understood what was expected of her. Surely she hadn't taken it so much to heart that she'd complained to his mother?

'I don't wish to make you fearful of me, Penny,' he said quietly. Quite the opposite in fact. 'I apologise if I gave any wrong impressions.'

'And so you should,' declared his mother strongly. 'I'm going to take a nap now. I'll leave you two to get better acquainted. And tonight we shall celebrate.'

Adam kissed her again, and watched as she walked into the house, and then he turned to Penny and smiled warmly, wanting to do more than that, fighting hard to restrain himself. 'Sit down, please.'

But already she was shaking her head. 'Your mother— she needs me. I usually—'

'I think that for once she will cope alone,' he told her firmly. 'Didn't you hear her? She wants us to spend time together; she wants us to become friends.' And he wanted to be more than friends—but he couldn't tell Penny that yet.

Adam Sterne was the last person Penny had expected to see. He never visited St Lucia, according to his mother. So why now?

Had it anything to do with her? Had he finally realised who she was? Was he here to send her back to England?

Her heart panicked, hammering painfully against her breastbone as she sat down and waited to hear what he had to say. Could this be the end before she'd even started? But when he did speak it was to say gently, 'You are happy here, Penny?'

She looked at him then in surprise. There was none of the envisaged hardness in his eyes, no rejection, merely concern. 'Yes, I'm happy.'

'My mother doesn't work you too hard?'

Penny frowned. This wasn't what she'd expected. 'Isn't that my job, to be kept busy by Mrs Sterne? But it's no hardship, I assure you. Who could take exception to working in this environment?'

'You're making good use of the pool?'

'Actually I haven't had time yet,' she told him truthfully. 'But—'

'Then my mother should be ashamed,' he declared, quite clearly shocked by her admission.

Penny allowed an eyebrow to lift delicately. 'You told me it was a twenty-four-hour-a-day job, Mr Sterne. I have no complaints.'

'Adam,' he corrected impatiently. 'And that doesn't mean to say that you can't have some leisure time. My mother always sleeps in the afternoon—what do you do with your time then?' He leaned forward and frowned ferociously into her face.

Penny shrugged. 'I usually sit in her room in case she wakes up and needs me.'

'And she lets you do that?' he asked in some astonishment.

'She's never commented on it.'

'Well, I think it's wrong,' he declared strongly. 'And I shall tell her so.'

He'd certainly changed his tune, thought Penny—from making a point of saying that she would have no spare time to insisting that she make use of the villa's leisure facilities. Was it because of the so-called attraction he had talked about? Was that the reason he was here? Not, as she had first suspected, because he knew who she was—but because he was interested in her as a woman?

Flames of heat licked along her nerves. Lord help her if that was the case. This man had destroyed her entire life.

She had gone to prison because of him.

'Foreman of the jury, do you find the defendant guilty or not guilty?'

'Guilty, my lord.'

Alexandra's gasp of disbelief was heard the whole court over. And when a sentence of six months was passed the whole world went black.

And all because Adam Sterne hadn't listened to her! Because he had taken the word of others. The mere thought of the horror and humiliation she had suffered was enough to snap her chin up and send a look of intense hatred in his direction.

She'd been released after three months for good behaviour, but it had been the longest three months of her life, the worst three months she'd ever experienced. That court-room scene would live in her memory for ever.

And this man sitting beside her now had had the power to stop it. It need never have reached court. All he'd had to do was to listen and believe.

But he'd chosen not to, and now he was reaching out a hand of friendship. How could she take it? How could she allow herself any feelings of warmth or pleasure where he was concerned?

'I'd prefer you said nothing to your mother,' she said, referring to his earlier comment. 'She'll think I've been complaining behind her back.'

'I rather got the impression that you'd been saying things about me?' A frown accompanied his words, and Penny knew he was wondering why she'd cast him such a scath-ing, frosty look.

She shook her head. 'I've said nothing.'

'So why does my mother think you're intimidated?'

'I don't know.' She lifted her shoulders and let them fall again. 'She has funny ideas sometimes.'

'Mmm,' he said reflectively, and then, with a swift change of subject, 'Why don't we go for a swim now?'

It was a reflex action to say, 'No, I couldn't.'

'Why not?' came the riposte.

Because I don't want you to see me half-naked, was her silent answer. Aloud she said, 'It wouldn't be right.'

'Because to all intents and purposes I'm your employer? Is that it? Like it wouldn't be right to call me Adam?' There was a thread of anger in his voice, quickly controlled. 'I think we can forget that, Penny. My mother's here on hol-iday, I'm here on holiday, so I think you should be too.'

Penny instantly shook her head. 'There are things she cannot do for herself.'

'Then we will share the duties,' he told her firmly. 'There's no earthly reason why you should tie yourself down completely now that I'm here. Go and put your swimsuit on.'

Penny went to her room, but not to undress. She sat on the edge of the pale jade bedcover and thought about the dilemma she now found herself in. Here was a man she both hated and found attractive. He was offering her the hand of friendship—probably more—and she didn't know what to do about it.

In reality she ought to walk out of here now, catch the first plane home. But she knew that she wouldn't do that. Something was holding her—and that something was not Lucy Sterne.

The only reason she'd taken the job was to find out more about Adam, to work out some way to wreak vengeance. An eye for an eye, didn't it say in the Bible? A tooth for a tooth.

Instead she felt a wildly impossible attraction. Instead of raking her nails down his face she wanted to kiss him. Instead of pummelling her fists on his chest she wanted to touch him, to feel the silken hardness of his skin. It was madness, it was sheer insanity, and yet the desire would not go away.

'Penny?'

Adam's voice reached her from outside the open floorlength window. 'Are you coming?'

'No, I've changed my mind,' she called out. 'You swim on your own.'

The next second the muslin drapes were pushed to one side and Adam stood there, tall and proud in brief black swimming trunks.

She couldn't help noticing how lithe and well muscled he was, how broad his shoulders, how narrow his hips. His skin was attractively tanned—despite the fact that his mother said he never took holidays—and the darkly curling hair on his chest was a temptation to her fingertips.

'I refuse to take no for an answer. Do I have to undress you myself?'

Penny closed her eyes, then opened them again quickly when she sensed rather than heard him step further into the room. 'OK, Adam, I'll swim with you.' He was but a short pace away from her. She fancied she could feel the warmth of him, and she could definitely smell his exciting male-ness.

Her breasts rose and fell as her breathing deepened, and Adam looked at them contemplatively for several long seconds, causing her nipples to harden and swell against the fine cotton of her dress.

She swung away. 'If you wouldn't mind leaving.' Damn the man. How dared he do this to her?

'Do you promise you'll be out in a few moments?'

'Yes.'

'Are you sure?'

'Of course I'm sure. Just go, Adam.'

She missed the smile on his face.

Hurriedly now she pulled on a black and white spotted swimsuit that she had bought especially for this holiday. It had been horrendously expensive, but worth every penny as the fit was superb.

Penny didn't realise how graceful and lovely she looked as she stepped out on to the verandah and down the step to the pool. She saw Adam's sleek dark head as he swam a leisurely breast stroke, and was glad he hadn't waited, glad he wasn't watching her approach.

She slid into the water and he swam to her side. Panic set in at the thought of him getting too close. 'Let's have a race,' she said quickly, and without waiting for his answer she pushed herself away from the side into a fast crawl.

They did ten lengths before she stopped, and although he beat her each time there was admiration on his face. 'You're quite a swimmer, Penny Brooklyn.'

'I was school champion,' she admitted as she hauled herself out.

'Congratulations. What else were you good at?'

She shrugged. 'I did well in most things, but I didn't excel in any one subject. I wonder if your mother's awake yet?' He was standing too close for comfort and she was anxious to get away.

'Don't worry about my mother. Maggie will see to her if she wants anything.'

'But—'

'But nothing. Come and sit in the shade.'

Reluctantly Penny followed him to where two loungers were positioned either side of a low table—he had clearly set them out earlier—and as soon as they were settled Maggie came out with a jug of iced orange juice.

'This is really a fabulous place,' she said, looking around her as he filled their glasses. The house sheltered two sides of the pool, and the extensive gardens with their smooth green lawns and endless flowering shrubs and trees fanned out on the other two sides. 'Your mother said you rarely come here. It seems such a pity.'

'Time is at a premium, Penny.'

Meaning time meant money, she thought bitterly. Making it was all he was interested in. 'Then why have you come now?'

There was a pause before he answered. A moment's space while he pushed her glass towards her and settled himself back on his lounger. 'I guess I finally felt I needed a break,' he said, watching her carefully through narrowed eyes.

'Or perhaps you're checking up on me? Making sure I'm doing my job properly?' The cutting rejoinder was out before she could stop it.

'Do you have a guilty conscience in that department?' he parried coolly, and then answered the question for himself. 'No, of course you don't. Anyone who sits with my mother while she sleeps when there's an inviting pool waiting out here has to have a conscience—a huge one at that. You're doing a good job, Penny.'

'Why, thank you, kind sir,' she said, looking at him over the top of her glass. The juice, freshly squeezed, was ice-cold and delicious, and she needed it to reduce her soaring temperature.

'What I can't understand,' he said, 'is why you're not married, why you don't even have a boyfriend.'

This reminder that he was the cause of her and Jon splitting up sparked fresh anger, and this she could deal with better than an unwanted attraction. 'I've not lived my entire life without a boyfriend,' she told him curtly. 'I was engaged at one time.'

'So what happened?' He sat up that little bit straighter and leaned towards her.

Penny swallowed hard. How she would love to tell him—but that would ruin everything. So she pulled a wry face. 'One of those things, I guess. He discovered that I wasn't the girl he thought I was.'

Eyebrows rose. 'You mean he dumped you? The man's a fool.' And then he smiled. 'On the other hand,' he said gruffly, 'maybe he did me a favour.'

'Did *you* a favour?' A painful thud in the region of her heart. More prickly heat on her skin. If he thought that he could start an affair with her then he was deeply mistaken. She would fight this attraction with every fibre of her being.

'If you hadn't been free then my mother would have been deprived of a very competent companion,' he pointed out.

His secretive smile suggested that he knew what she'd been thinking, and Penny deliberately avoided his all-seeing eyes, turning her attention back to her juice.

'And I wouldn't be sitting with you now,' he added softly, provocatively.

Penny kept her eyes on the glass, playing with the straw, wishing him a thousand miles away—or even four thousand. Then he would be back in England. And she would be safe.

'Do you mind?'

She frowned then. 'Mind what?'

'My being here.'

'Why should I mind?' she asked testily. 'It's your house; you can come and go as you please.'

'I suspect that you're not happy about it, though.'

'It was a shock,' she admitted.

'I was hoping it would be a nice one.'

'Why? What does it matter to you?' A leading question, and one she wished she hadn't spoken.

'Because,' he said slowly, 'as I said to you before, I—'

Penny knew what he was going to say, and in a desperate need to stop him she allowed the glass to slip out of her fingers. It dropped with a minor explosion on to the tiles.

'Oh, Lord, I'm sorry,' she said. 'I don't know how that happened.'

'Just stay where you are,' he ordered. 'I don't want you to tread in it. I'll get Maggie to clear up and bring you another glass.'

'It's all right,' she said, 'I don't want any more. I think

I'll go and take a shower and get dressed in case your mother needs me.'

'Damn my mother,' he grated. '*I* need you, Penny. Why the hell do you keep running away? I don't bite, you know.'

Penny forced herself to look at him. 'I'm aware of that, but I shouldn't be sitting out here relaxing when there's a job to be done.'

'Who's paying your wages?'

'You are,' she answered reluctantly.

'Therefore I wish you to spend some time with me.'

'Is that an order?'

A black scowl darkened his face. 'If that's the way you want to see it, yes. Personally I'd prefer the choice to be yours.'

So Penny stayed where she was. Maggie cleaned up and Adam poured her some more orange juice.

They sat in silence for a few moments, Penny with her eyes closed trying to pretend that Adam wasn't there. It was impossible. He was too dynamic a man, too sexy a man to ignore.

What she really wanted was to feast her eyes on him, to run them along the whole length of his body, up those long legs, those powerful thighs, over the flatness of his stomach, with the silky dark hair arrowing down into the waistband of his swim-trunks, across the powerful chest with yet more dark swirling hairs, finally reaching his strongly chiselled face with those sensual lips and those velvety dark brown eyes that could melt a woman on the spot.

'Do I pass muster?'

Red-hot heat scorched Penny's skin. She had not only been thinking it, she had been doing it! And he had seen her! How mortifying. How utterly, utterly stupid. 'I don't know what you're talking about.' Even her voice sounded shrivelled.

'Oh, I think you do. But if it's any consolation I enjoy looking at you too. You have a fantastic figure. I'm surprised you've never considered modelling.'

Modelling? That was a laugh. She'd been overweight most of her life. Bullied at school for being tall, she'd compensated for her unhappiness by eating chocolates and burgers and chips and everything that was unhealthy. Instead of making her feel better the weight that had piled on had made the bullying worse. And even when she'd left school and begun eating more sensibly the weight hadn't come off.

A spell in prison had done that for her. It was the only thing she could be thankful to him for.

To Penny's intense relief his mother chose that moment to walk out on to the verandah, smiling delightedly when she saw the two of them together. 'You've been swimming?' she said as she descended the steps to join them.

Adam pulled up a chair. 'Penny's an excellent swimmer. I had my work cut out to keep up with her.'

'You never told me that, dear,' said Lucy Sterne. 'Why haven't you used the pool before?'

'Because,' Adam answered for her, 'she took her duties too seriously.'

Lucy looked at Penny as though she didn't believe that, but she didn't pursue the subject, and after a few minutes' desultory talking Penny decided now would be a good time to take her leave.

Adam frowned, but didn't stop her, simply saying, 'Would you mind asking Maggie to bring a pot of tea out for my mother, and a plate of biscuits?'

Back in her room, Penny threw herself down on the bed. More than once she'd seen Adam looking at her with a speculative rather than a desirous look, and it worried her that he might recall where he'd seen her before.

It was unlikely, as they'd only ever spoken that once, but the fear remained, because she knew that instead of her getting even with him she would end up getting hurt again.

Dinner was a surprisingly pleasant meal, with Lucy insisting on champagne to toast the arrival of her adored son. But at nine o'clock she announced that she was going to bed.

Penny went with her, as normal, and hoped to be able to escape immediately afterwards. But Adam had other ideas. He appeared from nowhere the moment she stepped out of his mother's bedroom.

'I've been waiting for you. There's some champagne left. I wasn't looking forward to drinking alone.'

Penny ignored the treacherous quickening of her pulses. 'Actually, I was thinking of going to bed myself.'

'At this hour?' Well-shaped brows rose in disbelief.

'I've had a long day.'

'It won't hurt you to relax over a drink. We'll have it out on the sun deck. There's a breeze; it will be pleasantly cool.'

She was being given no choice. All she could hope was that he asked no searching questions.

The sun deck was a slatted wooden platform jutting out high over one corner of the pool. A rail ran round it for safety reasons. Set out on it were a table and two chairs. On the table the champagne nestled in a silver ice bucket, and beside it candles floated in a crystal water bowl.

It unnerved her, it looked like a seduction scene, but she refused to let her mind dwell on it. Instead she looked at the transformation that had taken place with nightfall. Pool-lights illuminated the water a clear aquamarine—it looked so inviting. Floor-lamps lit the pathways and cast mysterious shadows in the trees. 'It's wonderful,' she exclaimed, clapping her hands lightly. 'It's like a fairy grotto.'

He smiled at her enthusiasm. 'Didn't my mother ever put the lights on for you?'

Penny shook her head. 'She's always in bed early.'

'Then it's a good job I came,' he announced firmly. 'It would have been a pity if you'd missed this.'

He poured their champagne and Penny took her first sip, wrinkling her nose as the bubbles fizzed and popped.

She was wearing an ankle-length filmy cotton skirt and a short-sleeved top with a drawstring neckline, both in delicate shades of coral and ivory, and Adam had donned white linen trousers and a black half-sleeved shirt. She thought he looked gorgeous—and lethally dangerous too!

They were silent for a while, listening to the wind stirring the leaves of the palms and the giant tulip tree, *and her own heart thumping*! Penny didn't know what to say. She felt awkward in his company, and when Adam spoke she knew that she had been right to feel uneasy.

'Tell me about this boyfriend of yours, who cast you so cruelly to one side.'

CHAPTER FOUR

PENNY was tempted to blurt out, It was Jonathon Byrne, your technical director. He was another one who didn't believe I was innocent. But of course she didn't. She simply shook her head. 'I'd really rather not talk about him.'

'He hurt you that much, eh?'

'You can say that again,' she retorted strongly. But strangely enough she hadn't been totally heartbroken, simply angry and deeply hurt that he hadn't trusted her, hadn't believed in her.

Jon was the older brother of a girl with whom she'd started school. There was a four-year age-gap between them, but she and Emma had hung around with him nevertheless—when he'd let them! She could remember saying to him on her seventh birthday, 'I'm going to marry you when I grow up.'

When she was sixteen they'd started going out together, although it had taken him eight years to ask her to marry him. She had willingly agreed. It had been no blinding love affair; she'd never felt the electric sensations Adam Sterne had already managed to evoke. They'd simply been comfortable together, happy together, and she'd been content at the thought of setting up home with him.

These new feelings were a tremendous shock—this strong physical attraction. It was something she'd never experienced; it was exciting and frightening, and she couldn't imagine why it had happened under the circumstances.

'How long had you been going out together?'

Penny's eyes flashed her discontent. 'For ever. We grew up together.'

'You've had no other boyfriends?'

'No,' she answered, with a tiny shake of her head. She'd never looked at anyone else; she'd been happy with Jon. That was why his disloyalty had hurt so much.

She'd thought about him a lot while she was in prison, but they hadn't been fond thoughts. If the truth were known she hated him as much as she did Adam.

Adam's reaction was understandable—to a certain degree. Jon's wasn't. He knew her so well—how could he possibly have believed that she'd do such a thing? He hadn't even visited her. It was as though he'd washed his hands of her completely.

'When did he give you the heave-ho?'

At the same time as you sacked me, she retorted silently, bitterly, saying aloud, 'A few months ago.'

'So you're still raw and bleeding?'

Penny nodded. 'Perhaps you can see now why I don't want to talk about it.' She swallowed the rest of her champagne and held out her glass. 'Do you think I could have some more?'

He emptied the bottle, and with a smile in his voice said. 'I'd better get another.'

In the brief breathing space Penny leaned back and closed her eyes. It wasn't a good idea, sitting out here with him. It was too intimate, too magical. He must have known that when he suggested it, when he switched on the lights. Heaven alone knew what he had in mind. And would she be able to resist?

Even though he was no longer here she could still smell his aftershave, heady, exciting. Adam Sterne was definitely a full-blooded male—a male animal she ought to avoid at all costs!

'Here we are.' He slid into his seat and the hairs on the back of Penny's neck sensed danger. 'You're not going to sleep on me, are you?' he asked when he saw her closed eyes.

'I was just thinking how peaceful it is out here,' she lied. Peace was definitely not something she would ever associate with Adam Sterne. His presence was like a big, loud band playing inside her head.

'It's the perfect place to unwind.'

'And yet you rarely come here?'

'That's not strictly true,' he admitted, with a shameful twist of his lips. 'I do manage the odd holiday, usually tagged on at the end of some business trip. I don't tell my mother because, well, she'd ask too many questions.'

'Like who was with you?'

He nodded. 'She's anxious to see me married—actually, she's bemoaning the fact that she has no grandchildren.'

Which suggested that he *did* bring girls here. She wasn't the first to experience this wonderland, to be fêted with champagne. It was no surprise, and yet oddly it was a disappointment.

'Do you have a girlfriend at the moment?' Now why had she asked that? What a stupid question. It was no business of hers.

Adam's lips twitched. 'Are you really interested, or just plain nosy?'

Penny smiled. 'Nosy, I guess.'

'Like all women.'

She shrugged, still smiling because he didn't seem to mind.

'Actually, there's no one,' he finally admitted.

'Have you ever been married?'

He shook his head emphatically. 'When I marry, if I

marry, it will be for ever. I don't believe in divorce, quickie or otherwise.'

'So you've met no one you want to spend the rest of your life with?'

His face grew serious all of a sudden. 'There is someone, actually, but I'm afraid she's not in love with me.'

Had this woman seen the darker side of him too? wondered Penny. Had she been on the receiving end of his sharp tongue? It was the only reason she could think of why any woman would not fall in love with him. Because when he wasn't being arrogant and aggressive and totally abominable he was the perfect gentleman. He was caring, attentive and sensual.

'I'm sorry to hear that,' she said quietly. 'Is there no hope?' And was this the reason he was showing an interest in herself? Had he given up on this other woman?

His mouth twitched again. 'Let's say I'm working on it. More champagne?'

Penny was surprised to see that she'd already emptied her glass. She was drinking far more than she was used to and yet wasn't feeling light-headed. She allowed him to fill it up again.

'Forget me and my problems,' he said. 'Tell me more about yourself instead. Why didn't you like nursing?'

Penny shrugged. 'I don't think I was cut out to be a nurse. It was something I'd always wanted to do, but when it came to the crunch I didn't have the right aptitude.'

'So you took a course in design. Something totally different. You enjoyed that, I presume?'

'Very much.'

'It must have upset you a great deal when you were made redundant. Who was the company? Perhaps I know them.'

Penny took another long sip of champagne. 'I don't expect so. They're of no consequence.' And she actually meant that. As far as she was concerned Sterne Securities could sink to the bottom of the ocean, with everyone in it.

'Had they been in business long?'

Penny shrugged. 'Some years, I believe. I'm not sure.'

'And did you have an indication that you were going to lose your job?'

'None at all. It came as a monumental shock. One minute I was there, the next gone. I was devastated.' Penny did not realise that her voice had hardened, that her eyes were glinting with anger.

'How long ago was this?'

'About six months.'

His dark brows rose. 'At about the same time as your fiancé ditched you. No wonder you're bitter. Was there any connection?'

'I really don't wish to discuss it,' she told him firmly. 'It makes me very angry. If you can't find anything else to talk about then I'm going to bed.' She even set her glass down on the table.

As she did so Adam reached out, and would have taken her hand if she hadn't snatched it away. 'I don't like to see you upset,' he said. 'Let's take a walk around the garden, or even another swim. Whichever you prefer.'

Anything would be better than sitting here answering his questions, thought Penny. 'A walk, I think,' she said, and was down the steps before him.

In the velvety darkness of the night, with a dense silver canopy of stars above and the gentle glow of the garden lights at their feet, Penny wished she had chosen a swim. It was too romantic; Adam walked too close. Sometimes their arms brushed, and she would shoot away as a surge of heat passed through her.

The first couple of times it happened Adam said nothing, he was busy telling her the names of some of the flowers and shrubs, but when it happened a third time he came to an abrupt halt. 'What the hell is it that you've got against me?'

Penny's brows pulled together as she sought desperately for an answer. In the end she evaded the issue. 'I don't know what you're talking about.'

'I think you do,' he growled fiercely, 'but I'll spell it out so that we're both very clear.' He paused a moment, to make sure he had her full attention.

'If you're not looking at me as though you hate my very guts, you're shrinking away because you can't bear me to touch you—even accidentally. I've never been accused of being repulsive before, but I'm beginning to wonder.'

The glittering intensity in his eyes was like a punch in the stomach. 'You're not repulsive,' she said quickly, perhaps too quickly.

'Then what?' he demanded, eyes still stabbing, his mouth a thin, tight line.

Penny closed her eyes briefly. 'I—er—I—'

'You have no answer, do you?' he sneered, and he was once again the ruthless devil who had so callously dismissed her.

Penny's fingers curled tightly into her palms. She had an answer all right, but not one that she cared to give him right now. But one day—one day, yes—he would learn exactly what she thought of him.

'Perhaps I should prove to you that I'm not the monster you think I am.' He deliberately closed the gap between them. 'Perhaps I should—'

'No!' It was a cry of pure desperation. He *was* a monster. Nothing he could say or do would convince her otherwise. All it needed was a quick mental picture of cold iron gates closing, of a cellmate who drove her crazy, of the screams and cries of other women keeping her awake at night.

'No?' he asked gruffly, hands reaching out and urging her against the hardness of his body.

'No,' she breathed, holding the image.

Teeth gleamed in the parody of a smile. 'Let me warn you, Penny. I never take no for an answer.'

She could have moved, there was no real pressure, the lightest touch, but for some reason she didn't, couldn't. She remained within the circle of his arms, felt the heat of him, the long, hard length of his body pressing into the softness of her own, the unsteady beat of his heart.

Maybe it was the champagne. Maybe it was a combination of the drink, the incredibly romantic surroundings, and the totally drug-like scent of him.

Of their own accord her eyes lifted to his, and she felt herself being sucked into the deep, burning darkness, felt the faint tremble of his body, her own senses responding, turning to liquid, making her afraid of her own vulnerability.

She closed her eyes and waited for his kiss, knowing that it was inevitable, and was surprised to feel instead the touch of his fingertips across her face. So light, so gentle, so careful, tracing, feeling, maybe even committing to memory.

It was the way a blind man might do it, she thought, and she stood still and silent and allowed him to 'read' her face.

When his exploring fingers found and touched her lips desire began to make itself felt. Desire—she realised now—she had been holding in check for the last few seconds.

Her lips trembled and parted, and she was sorely tempted to moisten them with the tip of her tongue, to take his finger into her mouth, to suck, to press closer against him, to…

It was madness, sheer madness, and she made a tiny sound of protest.

'Shh,' said Adam soothingly. 'Shh.' And he began stroking her face again, while his other hand slid down the curve of her spine, slowly, slowly, as though he was counting each vertebra, settling finally on the small of her back.

Then, with his hand splayed, he gently pressed her even closer to him, so close that she could feel his desire—her own need fuelled and growing as she moved helplessly against him.

Quite when his lips replaced his fingers she did not know. The feathering of her face was still the same, still designed to arouse. It was only when his mouth closed over hers that awareness hit her.

She took breaths of air in little quivering movements, her body shuddering, but with pleasure not pain—pleasure that seeped through her veins with an impossible heat, pleasure that made her hands crawl up his back and come to rest on hard-muscled shoulders.

This was craziness, this was insanity, this wasn't what she wanted at all. So why wasn't she stopping him?

There was no answer. It was the headiness of the night, the expertise of the man, the crushing knowledge that her hatred might be forced to take a back seat. She would never dismiss it altogether, that was a fact, but for the few days he was here maybe...

His tongue moistened her lips in much the same way she had wanted to do earlier. Then he traced a finger across them, an incredibly erotic finger, which he put first into his own mouth and then into hers.

Jon had never made love to her like this. He had never tormented or teased, never created such a build-up of sexual awareness, sexual energy, desire. In fact he had never made love to her in the true sense of the words, declaring that he was old-fashioned and wanted to wait until they were married.

At the time she had thought it a truly wonderful virtue, had been proud of the fact that she was still a virgin. It was only now that she realised that Jon must never have truly loved her, that what they'd had was a strong friendship but nothing more. And even that had been found wanting!

And then Adam's tongue began to explore her mouth, finding its way slowly and erotically inside, tasting all the moist corners, tongue touching tongue, heartbeats matching heartbeats.

Penny heard a distant cry of pleasure and wondered where it had come from, before she discovered that *she* had made the noise, that she was uttering sounds of satisfaction, that she was urging herself closer to this devastatingly sensual man who was teaching her more about her own body in a few seconds than she'd discovered in the whole of her life.

Desire bled through her veins. She wanted more of what Adam had to offer, much more. When he lifted his mouth she instinctively shot her hands to his head, threading trembling fingers through crisp dark hair, pulling him back down.

'Penny?' He resisted at the last moment, just a fraction of a second before his mouth met hers. 'Is this truly what you want?' he asked hoarsely, two deep furrows chased into his handsome brow.

'Mmm.' It was all she could say. Demons were confusing her mind, making her want this man when she knew he was her enemy.

And so his mouth raided hers again, only this time he wasn't so gentle, this time he made no attempt to hide his hunger.

Nor did Penny.

It was a case of mutual need, a mutual invasion of each other's mouths. Penny could feel the echo of her pounding pulses in her ears, the equally damning throb of her heart, even Adam's heartbeat.

The sounds threatened to drown out the whole world, and it was with a tortured cry that she finally came to her senses. Her palms pushed desperately against his chest, felt the heat, the throb, the total maleness of him. 'No more. No more.'

Immediately he took a step back, a faintly derisory smile on his well-shaped mouth. 'Well, well, Miss Penny Brooklyn, you are a surprise. Who would have thought a few hours earlier that something like this would happen? Even a few minutes ago.'

Penny's head shot up. She tried to look disdainful but feared she failed. 'What do you mean? You were the one who started it.'

'You didn't stop me.'

'Would you have stopped?' she shot back. 'Something tells me that this whole thing was planned. The champagne, the candles, the subtle lighting. It was a seduction scene and I walked into it with my eyes closed.'

A smile twisted his lips. 'Closed? I think the lady lies. I also think that you're exaggerating the situation. It was never my intention to seduce you.'

Green eyes flashed. 'You're saying that you didn't want to kiss me?'

Another wry twist of his lips. 'I wouldn't go that far—you're an extremely fanciable lady—but I had nothing planned. I merely wanted to spend time with you, to get to know you a little better. And, correct me if I'm wrong, but you seemed to enjoy kissing me. You even pulled my head down to yours. If that doesn't tell me that you—'

Penny clapped her hands to her ears. 'I don't want to hear this. You must know that you're the type most women find hard to resist. But I've no intention of indulging in an affair while you're here.'

'Perhaps when you're back in England?' Dark brows rose hopefully.

'Not now, not ever,' she told him, furious both with him for kissing her and herself for being so weak. 'This is the one and only time I shall ever let you touch me. Call it a mental aberration, a moment of madness, or whatever you like—but it won't happen again.'

'You sound very sure about that. It's a pity. I quite enjoyed it.'

Damn the man. It had been a sensational experience as far as she was concerned, yet he'd only *quite enjoyed it*. If that wasn't a put-down then she didn't know what was. Of course, she mustn't forget that there was a woman somewhere whom he loved. He wouldn't have *quite enjoyed it* if he'd been kissing her. It would have been *wow!* and away with the stars.

'I'm going to bed,' she announced abruptly, and was more than a little annoyed when he fell into step beside her.

Although Adam was disappointed that Penny wanted to end the evening, and even more choked that the kiss had come to such an abrupt end, he had no intention of letting her see it.

He'd progressed well, considering he'd been here for only a few hours. The trouble was it had whetted his appetite. He wanted more, much more.

He remembered his mother, when he was a child and had craved a new TV for his bedroom, saying, 'Much wants more and greedy wants the lot.' It was true. He *did* want the lot. It was going to be difficult, if not impossible, to keep his hands off her.

'Are you always such an early bird?' he asked her now.

'I thought it was only my mother who went to bed while the night was still young.'

'I go when there's nothing else to do,' she told him sharply.

Adam winced, felt as though she'd kicked him in the stomach. Did kissing him count as nothing? Did his presence count as nothing? 'I thought you'd enjoy the night air. It's pleasant now, not so hot as earlier.' And why was he talking about the weather? It was an English pastime, yes, but not when he was with the girl of his dreams.

He was an idiot.

They should be talking about love.

'Then you stay and enjoy it.'

She spoke so coldly, so cuttingly, as though the kiss had never happened, as though he meant no more to her than a worm beneath her feet. Again it cut through him like a blast of icy air.

'I'm sorry if I've offended you.' Dammit, he seemed to spend all his time apologising to this girl. It wasn't the normal way of things. He was usually in control. Most things went the way he wanted them to.

He led a well-ordered life, if a busy one. He had worked hard to get where he was, and Sterne Securities now held an international reputation. There had been no hitches— except for that one occasion when some stupid girl in his design department had thought she could make herself a small fortune by selling his new system to one of his competitors.

She'd been tall too, but nothing like Penny. She'd been plump and unappealing, and had shuffled into his office in the most dowdy clothes imaginable, her long hair tied back in an unbecoming way, and she hadn't even held herself straight—as though she'd been embarrassed by her height.

He'd hardly looked at her—he'd done what he'd had to do and then dismissed her.

He liked beautiful women—smart, sophisticated women. Women like Penny. Yes, Penny. He glanced at her now, walking so tall and proud at his side. 'Haughty' was the word that sprang to mind.

He was intrigued. She'd been right when she'd said that not many women resisted him. Not that he played around. There had been the odd woman he'd taken a fancy to—but none had got beneath his skin like Penny Brooklyn.

'You've not offended me,' she said, in answer to his earlier comment. 'It's what I might have expected.'

He waited for the *from someone like you*. But it didn't come, and he guessed she'd bitten back the words.

'Why do you have such a low opinion of me?' he asked quietly, wondering whether she had any idea how much it hurt. Lord, he wanted to touch her, at least hold her hand, but knew that he didn't dare, that he had to tread gently from now on.

'What makes you think I have?' came the defensive response.

'I'd need to be blind not to see it. Or is it that since your boyfriend let you down you're shutting men out of your life altogether?' If that was so then he stood a good chance. It would be a pleasure persuading her that she was making a mistake.

On the other hand, if she was tarring the whole male sex with the same brush then convincing her that she had a future with him would be a lot harder. If she'd vowed to let no one in then she must be really angry with herself now for her temporary lapse. The door to her heart would be padlocked and double bolted, and she would do everything in her power to make sure it stayed that way.

'You could say that,' she answered. 'I don't have much

faith in men at the moment—nor am I ever likely to,' she added bitterly. And still she marched on.

They were entering the house now, and Adam wondered how far he dared go with her—to her bedroom door? Would that be acceptable? Somehow he didn't think so. But he didn't want to let her go any sooner than he had to.

'Can I get you a nightcap?'

'No, thank you. I think I've drunk more than enough already.' She stopped and turned, and flashed her beautiful eyes at him. 'Like you, Mr Sterne, I like to be in control.'

He wasn't quite sure what she meant by that, and he sure as hell didn't like the *Mr Sterne* bit, but he let it go. 'A hot drink, then? Chocolate? Something malted?' Please, anything so that you'll stay a few minutes longer.'

'Your persistence is admirable, but I'd think more of you if you took no for an answer.' Another flash of those gorgeous green eyes, then she turned and walked away.

He let her go.

What else could he do?

He poured himself a Scotch, and then another, and it was the early hours before he went to bed. He didn't sleep; he hadn't expected to. His mind was filled with tantalising images—of Penny in her swimsuit, of her long, slender body poised as she dived into the pool, of the feel of her against him, the taste of her mouth, the joy when she had held his head close—the hope so swiftly dashed.

He was up early, swimming before breakfast, hoping Penny would join him, disappointed when she didn't. But his hopes were lifted again when his mother, who put in an unusual appearance for breakfast, suggested that he and Penny go out for the day.

'I'm still recovering from yesterday,' she said, trying to look languid, when in fact she looked highly excited.

There were spots of high colour in her cheeks, and both

he and Penny would have had to be blind not to see that she was deliberately pushing the two of them together.

'I couldn't leave you,' said Penny at once, as he'd guessed she would. But he knew that his mother was more than a match for this darling woman, and was content to let her sort out their plans.

'Nonsense, child. I have Maggie if I need anyone. But I suspect that I shall sleep for most of the day.'

'Aren't you feeling well, Mrs Sterne?' asked Penny, her green eyes shadowed with concern.

'I feel as fit as a fiddle—always do when I'm out here,' the older woman announced firmly. 'But that doesn't mean I don't need my rest. If you don't go, Penny, I shall be very cross. You've given so much of your time to me that you deserve a break. Adam's arrival has been most fortuitous.'

Good old Mother, he thought, and looked at Penny. The two women were at opposite ends of the table and he sat between them. Watching them as they spoke was a bit like a tennis match. Come on, Penny, he thought, your serve.

It was with reluctance that she finally gave a small nod. 'You win, Mrs Sterne. Though I must tell you that I'm not happy about it. I'm here to look after you, not to go out with your son.'

'I wouldn't be telling you to go, child, if I felt I needed looking after. And, never fear, it won't be a daily occurrence.'

A pity, Adam thought. He could easily get used to the idea of squiring Penny around. It was a start, though, and one he intended taking every advantage of. Already in his mind he was wondering where to take her, and a smile crossed his face as he thought of the ideal place.

CHAPTER FIVE

WHEN Adam had advised her to put on a pair of good walking shoes Penny hadn't minded, because she loved walking, but when he'd also suggested she bring her swimsuit she'd felt uneasy.

She had no intention of getting into any more compromising situations. And swimming together, semi-naked bodies, awareness, almost certainly touching, was compromising to say the least.

If she hadn't thought that it would hurt Lucy Sterne's feelings she would have told her quite emphatically that she didn't want to go with Adam. And now, sitting in his hired Mercedes, feeling the full impact of his devastating sensuality, she knew that she'd been right to feel apprehensive.

'Enjoying yourself?'

The deep sexy timbre of his voice sent more pulses racing, added to the turmoil already created by such close proximity.

Instead of answering, instead of lying and saying, yes, of course she was, Penny said, 'Where are we going? Fabian showed us the island yesterday.'

'But he wouldn't have taken you to this place.' Adam glanced across and smiled. 'If he had he'd have had to carry my mother.'

Penny smiled too at the thought of the prim Lucy Sterne in Fabian's arms.

'We're going on a hike which starts at the botanical gardens in Soufrière.'

They'd just passed through Castries, so, if she remembered correctly, it was about another half hour's drive away. The whole island was only twenty-seven miles by fourteen, but the roads were nothing like the motorways of England and it took a lot longer to get anywhere. In any case Adam was taking his time, giving her every opportunity to look around.

'We went to the gardens,' she told him, wondering why he'd said bring a swimsuit if they were going walking. Unless, of course, he planned to take her to the ocean afterwards. 'There are some incredible plants there, some really beautiful ones—the sort we never see in England. But your garden is lovely too. Fabian does an excellent job looking after it.'

'Indeed. We were lucky to find him and Maggie. Did you sleep well last night?'

Damn! Why did he have to change the subject? Why did he have to bring personal issues into it? She'd been coping, just, while they were talking about the island, but now she grew aware of him again, felt her senses disturbed, felt the full impact of his sensuality.

'Yes, I did,' she lied. 'Wonderfully well.' There was no way she was going to admit that she'd lain awake most of the night thinking about him.

That kiss had done so much damage. She felt wounded by it, felt that the scars would never go away, would never heal. She only had to close her eyes and she could feel his mouth on hers, his tongue touching, tasting, exploring, exciting.

What madness it had been letting him do it—and how hard it would be to stop him if he tried again. The kiss had been like a taste of forbidden fruit, a taste so sweet and succulent, so enticing, that she knew she would crave it for evermore.

That was why she had walked away, why she had fought against going out with him today—not that it had got her anywhere. His mother had seen to that. Adam himself hadn't said a word, but she'd read the smug expression on his face. It couldn't have worked out any better as far as he was concerned.

'I'm glad to hear you had a good night,' he said. 'You'll need all your energy.'

Penny wondered what was in store. She had her swimsuit on beneath a pair of denim shorts and a cotton T-shirt, and she had socks and trainers on her feet. She hadn't bothered with a towel because she knew she would dry quickly in the heat of the sun.

She had carefully lathered herself with high-factor sun-screen, and all she carried was a linen shoulder bag with more cream and a comb and a few tissues.

When they reached Soufrière and began their walk she stopped worrying and started to enjoy herself. 'This is the Morne Coubaril Estate,' Adam told her, 'and normally you'd go with a special guide, but we'll dispense with that today.'

Meaning he wanted to keep her to himself, thought Penny. But when Adam pointed out a cocoa tree, with its dark, strangely shaped pods, she was so intrigued she forgot her animosity. He picked one of the pods and cracked it open, and when she tasted the sweet pulp which coated the cocoa beans she was glad he'd brought her. These were things she would never experience again.

The trail went upwards, following the Coubaril stream, and as they walked Adam made sure she saw the papaya trees, the pineapples and bananas, the orange and grapefruit trees, all peeping out through the dense vegetation of this lush green rainforest.

It was a rare wonderland as far as Penny was concerned.

She kept stopping and looking and exclaiming, especially when she thought she saw a parrot. And the longer they trudged the hotter she got. Perspiration poured freely, and she could have flung her arms around Adam when he produced cool drinks from a rucksack on his back. 'You're a lifesaver,' she declared.

And then it was on and up again, and just as she was beginning to feel that she could go no further, when her legs felt like lead, when the sweat was running in rivers down her back and between her breasts, and she wanted nothing more than to lie down and rest, they arrived at their destination.

'The Coubaril Falls,' announced Adam with some satisfaction. 'What do you think?'

Penny looked up at the Falls, and then down to where they cascaded into a rock pool. They were spectacular, but what interested her more were the people in the pool, people who stood beneath the welcoming jets of water. Now she knew why he'd suggested her swimwear.

'I can't wait,' she said with a wide smile, and began tearing off her T-shirt and shorts, hopping from foot to foot as she kicked off her shoes. But her biggest surprise came when she entered the water.

'Adam?' she enquired, her eyes wide and questioning. 'It's warm!'

He too had worn trunks beneath shorts and shirt, and it had been a race to see who'd get in first. Now he smiled at her surprised expression.

'It's fed by volcanic sulphur springs,' he told her, 'and the closest thing you'll ever get to a hot shower in the forest.'

'It's wonderful,' she exclaimed, finally feeling completely relaxed with him. She had been to the volcano yesterday, proudly boasted as being the only drive-in volcano.

The smell of sulphur had been very strong, and pools of boiling water had bubbled merrily away. 'I wish you'd told me what to expect.'

'And spoil the surprise?'

She turned her face up to the water and let it pour over her.

'The sulphur is said to be very good for your skin,' he informed her, 'and some people believe it helps relieve arthritis.'

'Then you should bring your mother here,' she retorted. But they both knew that was impossible.

Penny hadn't really noticed the other people drifting away—until suddenly she and Adam were alone. 'It's like we're the only two people in the world,' she said. And surprisingly she didn't mind. She didn't feel in the least intimidated by him. 'This is such a magical place, Adam, I'm so glad you brought me here.'

'I thought you'd like it. It's an experience not to be missed. I always come whenever I'm on the island.'

'Alone?'

His lips twisted wryly. 'Sometimes. I brought a girlfriend once, but when she realised that she'd get her hair wet she refused to come in. Needless to say the relationship didn't last. I can't stand women who fuss over their appearance to that extent.'

'It was probably because she didn't want you to see her hair in a mess,' said Penny. 'We women have our pride, you know.'

'There's nothing more beautiful than a woman's hair when it's hanging soaking wet over her shoulders, showering her body with diamond-like droplets of water. Why do you keep yours so short?'

Penny hadn't expected that, and she lifted her shoulders,

trying to look indifferent. 'I used to wear it long. I wanted a change.'

'If you were mine I would make you grow it again.'

'Make me?' He was good company today and she was relaxed enough to tease him.

'Yes, make you, you little green-eyed witch.' His smile was wide, his teeth very white. 'You look like a boy at the moment—except for…' He glanced down at her rounded, taut breasts, but only very briefly, nothing to embarrass her, and she laughed.

'I can assure you, Adam Sterne, that I'm definitely not a boy.' They were separated at this moment by the curtain of water, and she felt relatively safe.

It was a unique experience, showering in this warm, sulphurous water, and all her aches had gone. She felt revitalised, and was almost feeling sad at the thought that they would soon be wending their way back down.

'Do you think I'd be here with you if you were? You're one hell of an exciting woman.' He looked at her long and hard, and she thought he might be about to kiss her, but instead he stepped out of the Falls and sat on a rock at the edge of the pool.

'Have you had enough?' she called.

'We're about to have company,' he told her. 'I can hear people making their way up.'

Because of the thunderous noise of the water Penny hadn't heard anything, but in seconds a whole crowd of people came into sight, and she was disappointed that their few minutes' idyll was about to be disrupted.

She joined him on the rocks, which had been discoloured by the minerals in the water—green, mustard-yellow, and even deep red. They sat there until they were dry, watching the newcomers, not speaking much, simply enjoying being there. She was totally relaxed with him now.

They dressed soon afterwards, and Adam produced another can of cola and a chunk of fresh coconut, and then they were off again. Instead of going down, though, they carried on climbing.

The track was steeper, and quite slippery because of recent rain, but there was rope strung in places to hold on to, and steps cut into the hillside to make climbing easier.

Adam went in front, but he kept turning and checking and asking whether she was all right.

'I bet your girlfriend with the hair didn't do this,' she said with a grin.

He chuckled. 'You're right. It was straight back down after the Falls. But there's a restaurant at the top, and the view over Soufrière is well worth the climb.'

His dark hair had fallen across his forehead and he was beginning to sweat. Up until now the climb hadn't seemed to bother him, so Penny was glad to see that he was suffering too.

Because suffering she was. The backs of her legs ached with the unaccustomed climbing, her throat felt as though it was sticking together, and she was as wet with perspiration as she had been from the waterfall. 'How much further?' she asked, after they'd been going for three-quarters of an hour.

'Not long now—about fifteen minutes. Do you want to rest?'

'Please.'

And so they stopped, and she leaned against a palm while he fished two more cans out of his rucksack. The drink was warm, but that didn't matter. It went down Penny's throat like nectar.

'You're an incredible girl.'

'Am I?' Green eyes widened. 'Why?'

'Because you've never once complained.'

'What's to complain about? I'm really enjoying myself, despite the fact that my legs feel ready to drop off,' she added with a laugh.

He frowned his concern. 'You should have told me you wanted to rest.'

'And have you call me a wimp?'

An eyebrow rose. 'I don't think I'd ever do that.' And he inched closer towards her. 'Have I told you that I like tall women?'

Oh, no, please don't start anything, she implored silently. Don't spoil things. I'm having such a good time. But she kept her feelings hidden and said cheekily, 'That's because you're tall yourself. You'd have a bad back if you went out with a five-feet-nothing woman.'

'True. I tried it once. I thought this protective male thing would shoot in, but it didn't; it was damned awkward.' He laughed at the memory. 'Are you ready to move on?'

Penny nodded, relieved the moment had passed.

After a few more minutes' walking, he called, 'Not far now.'

And because she looked up as he spoke, taking her eyes off the uneven path, Penny caught her toe on a boulder and pitched helplessly forward, ending up in a sprawling heap on the stony path.

Her cry brought Adam instantly to her side, real concern on his face. 'What happened? Are you hurt?' he asked as he helped her up.

'No, I don't think so. It was just so stupid. I didn't look where I was going. Ouch!'

'What?' he asked immediately, his hand beneath her elbow.

'It's my ankle. I think I might have sprained it a little.' She tested it again on the ground. 'No, it's not too bad; I can manage. Ouch!'

'Manage be damned,' he growled. 'We're almost at the top. I'll carry you.'

'I'm no lightweight,' she warned. 'Maybe if I could just lean on your arm?'

But he would have none of it. He swung her up as though she were a child and strode the rest of the way without a falter in his step.

Although Adam was being completely impersonal a buzz ran through Penny that she couldn't dismiss. She wanted to link her arms around his neck and kiss him, to feel once again that firm mouth on hers, to taste him, to enjoy.

It was total insanity. A few days ago she'd wanted to stick a knife in his back—and now this! What the hell was happening to her? Why was she so weak where this man was concerned?

At the restaurant he sat her down, wrapped a cold wet bandage around her ankle, and told her to stay where she was while he fetched the car. It was a relief to know they hadn't got to walk back down, because she knew she'd never have made it.

And when he finally got her home he fussed over her like a mother hen: carrying her indoors, settling her on one of the squashy sofas with her feet up, changing the bandage for a fresh cooling one, bringing her a drink and saying Maggie would have food ready in a short time.

'Adam, stop it,' she protested fiercely. 'It's nothing, just a bit of a sprain. I don't need looking after like this.'

'A bit?' he asked scornfully. 'Look how it's swollen. You'll need to keep your weight off it for several days at least.'

'But your mother,' she said at once. 'I can't do that. She—'

'My mother will be looked after. Don't worry so much.'

Penny grimaced. 'I'm so sorry,' she said. 'I feel such a fool.'

'Then you're a delightful fool,' he told her. 'I'm simply grateful that it's no worse.'

'I spoilt the day.'

'There'll be other times.'

'I was really enjoying it.'

'Does that mean you're beginning to like me?' An eyebrow curved, brown eyes twinkled, his lips twitched. 'Am I making progress at last?'

She couldn't help smiling in return. 'Maybe, just a little bit.' It would be fatal to tell him how much.

'But I still have to tread cautiously?'

She avoided answering by saying, 'I wish *I* had, then I wouldn't be in this predicament.'

He grinned, showing once again those amazingly white teeth. 'Do you know what? I think I'm going to enjoy looking after you.'

He looked so boyish when he smiled, thought Penny, so different, so approachable, so—lovable! And she would have to be careful. This wasn't in her plan of things at all.

Think prison, she told herself sternly. Think of the humiliating strip search, of the bars at the windows, of the obnoxiousness of some of the other inmates—especially the one who shared your cell.

It was enough to tighten her face, to wipe all the loving feelings from her body. 'I don't think that will be necessary,' she said coolly.

He looked at her, gave his head a tiny shake. 'Have I missed something here?'

'What do you mean?'

He spread his hands helplessly. 'You've suddenly changed. What little progress I've made has gone. We're back to square one. Why?'

'Maybe I've just remembered that you're my boss. Ah, here's Maggie. I'm starving.' The woman couldn't have come at a more opportune moment.

'You all right, Miss Penny?' the woman asked as she piled cushions behind her back and placed the tray of food on her lap. 'You should be more careful.'

'I know,' she admitted. 'But it's done now. I'll try not to be a nuisance.'

Maggie smiled. 'You could never be that.'

And then, to Penny's dismay, she fetched another tray for Adam and he perched on the end of the sofa.

'I'm sure you can't be comfortable there,' she said. 'Why don't you eat at the table?'

'You mean you don't want me near you?' he asked, with a sneer in his voice which she hated to hear. 'If so I'm going to disappoint you, because I've no intention of moving. There are a few things that you and I need to sort out.'

'Such as?' she asked, taking a forkful of deliciously tender dorado, only to find that the fish tasted like cardboard. Nothing to do with Maggie's cooking, just her own throat refusing to swallow. Why couldn't Adam go away again, and leave her and his mother to enjoy the holiday alone? Why had he spoilt it?

'This sudden change of heart, for instance.' His eyes raked her face as he spoke. 'And don't give me that boss nonsense because I don't believe it. You even admitted only seconds ago that you were enjoying my company. What the hell happened?'

The fish wasn't sticking in his throat; he ate hungrily as he waited for her answer. Penny didn't look at him. She forked the fish around on her plate, tried another tiny mouthful, and managed to force it down.

'I'm waiting, Penny.' And it sounded as though his patience was running out.

'There's nothing to say.' She finally looked at him, and winced inwardly as hard dark eyes pierced hers. If he hadn't been the man he was it could all have been so different, so very, very different.

'I think there is,' he snorted. 'There has to be a reason for your mood swings.'

She lifted her shoulders and let them drop again. 'It's the sort of person I am.'

'I don't think so,' he said tersely. 'I think you're afraid of showing your emotions. I think that rat of a fiancé did a really good job on you. You almost forgot yourself for a short while, but now the defences are back in place. I'm right, aren't I?'

Penny closed her eyes and slowly nodded. It was best he believed this.

'You can't let it ruin your life.'

'I need more time.'

'Hell, how much time? It's been—what?—well over six months, for God's sake. It's time you started living again, Penny.' He put his tray down on the floor, hers too, then kneeling at her side, he took her hands into his and looked deeply into her eyes.

'Whoever this guy is he needs whipping for deserting you in your hour of need. But we're not all the same. I would never do such a thing. I'd be there with you, helping you find another job, and there are thousands of others like me. You have to believe that.'

She shook her head. How could he say that he'd never hurt her? He'd had the power to save her. And yet all he'd done was listen to others; he'd not allowed her to say one word in her own defence. He'd thrust the onus on the courts.

With damning consequences!

Her lips tightened. 'I can't believe it.'

'Can't, or stubbornly won't? Dammit, woman, why punish yourself for something that he did? I wish you'd tell me who he is; I'd like to ring his bloody neck.'

And still he held her hands.

'There's nothing you can say or do,' she said quietly. 'Please leave me alone.'

'I can't.'

Her eyes widened. 'What do you mean, you can't?'

'You've got beneath my skin, woman. I can't sit by and let you suffer like this. I have to do something.'

'And that something means holding my hands, touching me, kissing me, possibly even wanting to make love to me? Is that what you're saying? Is that your definition of helping?' The words came tumbling out and she couldn't stop them.

With a swift movement he let her go, shaking his head as he sprang to his feet. 'That's not what I meant at all, dammit, although I'm not saying that I haven't thought about it. You're a hell of a sexy woman when your hackles aren't up. But I think you're right. I think I should leave you. Leave you to come to your senses!' He gave her one last final, furious glare before he marched from the room.

Never in his life had Adam met a woman as confusing as Penny Brooklyn. What game she was playing he didn't know. One moment he thought he was getting somewhere with her, the next she was shutting him out, retreating into her ice-cold shell and wanting nothing to do with him.

For pity's sake, he wasn't after an affair, he didn't want to take her to bed—he'd settle for the hand of friendship. And who was he trying to kid? Friendship to start with, yes, but more than that ultimately. He wanted her body and soul. He wanted her to be his wife.

On the way to his bedroom, thoughts tossing impatiently

around in his mind, he met his mother. Maggie had said she was asleep, after an early lunch, and he wished she still was. He didn't want the third degree.

'Adam, what are you doing back so soon?' she asked with a frown. 'You look worried to death. Is something wrong?'

Yes, my heart's bleeding. The woman I love wants nothing to do with me. But of course he didn't say these words. 'Penny's hurt her ankle,' he volunteered instead.

'Not badly, I hope?' Her pale eyes were full of instant concern.

'No, just twisted it a bit. But she'll need to rest for a day or two.'

'I must go to her. Where is she? And why on earth did you let it happen? Weren't you looking after her?' There was sharp condemnation in her tone.

'Mother! Of course I was looking after her. These things happen, you know. We did the climb above Coubaril Falls and she slipped. It was no one's fault. She's on the sofa in the living room.'

'Why aren't you with her?'

'I've only just left, Mother,' he said, trying to contain his patience. 'But she wouldn't eat her lunch. See if you can persuade her.'

Tutting loudly, Lucy Sterne headed for the living quarters, her walking stick tapping rhythmically on the white-tiled floor.

Adam went to his room.

He tried telling himself that all it required to win Penny's trust was patience. But he'd never been a patient man. He was prepared to work towards a goal if he could see that an end was in sight, but if there was no hope—or it seemed that there was no hope—then his patience ran very thin.

With an angry gesture he tossed off his shirt and headed

for the pool, but it took twenty racing lengths before he felt any better. Then resolve took over. He would prove to Penny that he was different, that she could trust him, that he would never let her down.

He wouldn't demand anything of her that she didn't want to give, he would be gentle, caring, not too attentive, to frighten her away, but he would be there for her when she needed someone.

The odd thing was he hadn't said anything to upset her when the barriers had come up. He'd simply said that he would enjoy looking after her. She must have read more into it than he'd meant, panicked, perhaps, and the next second he was left out in the cold.

He might even—once they became friends, *if* they became friends—offer her another job when this one was finished. He could use someone with her qualifications. That Brooke woman's replacement wasn't working out. She didn't have the right attitude—according to Donna.

He'd gained the impression that Donna hadn't approved of Alex Brooke either, but until she'd fouled up by trying to line her own pockets he'd had no complaints about her work. In fact from what he'd seen of it she was very good.

But it would help Penny if she knew that she had another job lined up. It couldn't be any fun being out of work—downright humiliating, in fact, having to sign on the dole.

Feeling better now that he'd made a decision, Adam hauled himself out of the pool and flopped on a lounger—and there he intended staying until it was time to get ready for dinner.

It was best that he keep out of Penny's way for a while, give her time to rationalise her thoughts. Then, over dinner, with his mother's watchful eye on her, she would be compelled to be pleasant to him.

But Penny wasn't present at dinner. 'She's having her

meal in her room,' declared his mother. 'I think her ankle's worse than she's letting on. Maybe you ought to call a doctor.'

Adam frowned. 'How did she get there? I hope she didn't walk. I told her to—'

'Fabian.'

'Why didn't you call me?' he asked sharply, resentfully. Wasn't he the obvious choice?

'Penny didn't want to bother you,' his mother said evenly. 'You looked as though you were sleeping. I can't help but notice that you both seem a bit strained.'

Adam winced inwardly. The last thing he wanted was his mother asking questions. 'There's nothing wrong. I'm worried about her, that's all.'

'And Penny?'

'I expect it's her ankle.'

'Hmmpf,' sniffed his mother, clearly not believing him, but not wanting to call him a liar either.

'I'll look in on her when we've finished.'

But when he did so, when he pushed open the door and stepped inside, she took one look and ordered him out. 'When are you going to accept that I don't want you around me?' she blazed. 'Do us all a favour and go back to England.'

CHAPTER SIX

HAD Penny any idea how much her words hurt? wondered Adam. Didn't she know that he wanted to help her get over her crisis? She needed help. She must not be allowed to let one man ruin her life for evermore.

He could have walked away, done as she'd said, but that wasn't what he wanted to do. 'Penny,' he said gently, 'I hope you don't mean that. I have your best interests at heart. Is your ankle unbearable? If so, then—'

'No, it isn't,' she slammed back. *'You're* the unbearable one.'

He sucked in a deep breath. She was so cruel at times, and yet stunningly beautiful in her anger. Her lovely green eyes were flashing points of light at him, there was high colour in her cheeks—and the tray of food before her was untouched!

'I still can't understand why you feel that way about me,' he said reasonably. 'I assure you, Penny, I'm not about to—'

'I don't care what your intentions are,' she flared. 'I don't want you here.'

'Not even if they're honourable?' Lord, he wanted to shake her—shake some sense into her. Didn't she realise that she was hurting herself as much as him?

'Not even if you write them down in your own blood,' she thrust icily.

Adam closed his eyes and shook his head. It was beginning to look as though there was no way through to her, that she had built an impregnable wall.

He had known from the start, from the interview, that she was against him. She had struggled hard not to show it, but her feelings had crept through. He'd not paid it too much attention because his main concern had been that she was suitable for his mother. But maybe he should have been warned.

And again, when he'd fetched her on the morning of the flight, she had sat as far away from him as possible, hunching herself against the door—and then said there was nothing wrong when he'd asked.

These little things added up.

'Perhaps you're forgetting,' he said, 'that this is *my* villa. There is no way you can throw me out.'

She looked not in the least abashed. 'OK, so *I'll* go—as soon as my ankle's better.'

'You'd turn your back on my mother, when she's come to rely on you?'

Her eyes blazed. 'You're here, you're used to her, you do it.'

He looked at her for a few long, taut seconds. Perhaps a kiss would do the trick? Most women he'd dated had been putty in his hands if he'd so much as touched them. And Penny had responded once, why not again?

But he knew she wouldn't. She had erected those damned fences and nothing was going to knock them down. She would more likely slap his face. And his chances of ever forming any sort of relationship would be lost for ever.

'You think my mother would accept that?' he enquired coolly. 'She knows I can't afford to take three months off. If you go home then my mother will go as well. It's as simple as that. You'll be depriving her of a much needed holiday.'

He hated blackmailing her but it seemed the only way.

Her mouth was mutinously set, her green eyes glittering, her unsteady fingers pleating the edges of the sheet.

Finally she heaved a long, shuddering sigh. 'You give me no choice. I should hate to let your mother down. But I insist that you keep away from me for the rest of the time that you're here.'

'What do you think my mother would say if I ignored you?' he asked calmly, not wanting to let her see that he was rattled, that she was hitting him where it hurt most. 'She's already asked me if there's anything wrong. She's not an idiot, Penny. She doesn't go around with her eyes closed.'

He watched the grimace that screwed up her eyes, stretched her lips, and found that he was holding his breath for her answer.

'Very well,' she accepted with ill grace, 'we'll pretend—in front of your mother. But at any other time, forget it.'

'And you think she'll be convinced?' he asked wearily. 'She hasn't seen us together today, and yet she knows there's tension between us. You'll have to do better than that.'

'I can't.'

'Can't, or won't?'

Another heavy sigh, another sullen stare. 'Don't blame me if it doesn't work.'

Victory was his! Why, then, wasn't he feeling jubilant? Because he knew that it was still going to be an uphill struggle. She had conceded, but with ill grace, and probably with no intention of relaxing in his company.

'Why don't you eat your dinner?' he asked softly, taking a further step into the room.

'I'm not hungry.'

'You hardly touched your lunch. Is it not to your liking? Can I get you something else?'

Penny thought for a moment. 'Yes. I'd like fish and chips, from a chippie. I've missed them since we left England.'

He allowed himself to smile. 'I can't oblige with a fish and chip shop, and I'm not sure it's on Maggie's menu. But if that's what you want, then that's what you shall have.'

He lifted the tray, controlling the urge to touch her, to brush his hand across her cheek, *to tell her he cared.* Instead he contented himself with inhaling the sweet, intoxicating scent of her womanly body. It would have to do for the time being.

When he had gone Penny slumped wearily against the pillows. It had been a hard-fought battle but she'd won. Well, not entirely, but Adam hadn't had all his own way, and hopefully he'd got the message and would respect her wishes.

So why wasn't she deliriously happy? Why, when he'd taken the tray, had she wanted him to lean down and kiss her? She'd fought to keep him at arm's length, to maintain a strictly platonic relationship; she ought to be on top of the world.

A frightening sort of truth crept in. One she didn't dare admit even to herself. It couldn't be. It wasn't possible. No! No, no, no.

She spent the next half an hour or so refusing to give the thought access, and when Adam returned, with her requested fish and chips, she wasn't sure that she could eat them.

But if she didn't he would ask questions, so she forced a smile and allowed him to stack the pillows behind her back, holding her breath when his arm brushed her shoulders, trying not to tense herself but aware that she did. Aware also that his lips tightened.

'There we are,' he said. 'Comfy now?' Nothing in his voice to suggest that he was aware of her tension.

'Yes, thank you,' she said quietly.

The fish and chips looked delicious: fat chips, golden crispy batter on the fish, even mushy peas and thinly sliced bread and butter. Not huge portions, just a tempting amount, and once she'd taken a mouthful Penny was surprised how much she enjoyed it. She didn't even object when Adam sat on a chair and watched her.

'Is it good?' he asked at length.

'Delicious. Tell Maggie she must definitely keep it on the menu from now on.'

'Maggie didn't cook it.'

Penny lifted questioning brows. 'So who did?'

'Me.'

'You?'

'Don't look so surprised. I've had many years' experience. First of all as a student, cooking on a budget—you'd be amazed at the combinations. I must have had an iron gut. And then when I bought a house of my own I quite enjoyed playing the domestic.'

'Did you have to sell your house when your father died and your mother needed you?'

'I didn't have to, but I did.'

'Were you sorry?'

'In one respect, but Whitestone Manor's big enough for me to have total independence.'

'Where was your house?'

'In York.'

'Oh, I love York,' she said impulsively. 'I love the Minster, and the Walls, and everything about it. I love old places.'

'But it's not always practical living in them,' he pointed out. 'It costs a small fortune to run Whitestone Manor, for instance. It swallows up money like parched earth soaks up rain.'

'Your mother obviously doesn't mind, or she'd move somewhere smaller.'

'My mother thinks things cost the same as they did twenty years ago,' he informed her drily. 'She's out of touch with reality. My father protected her and I guess I've been doing the same ever since.'

I'd like you to protect me. It was a thought that came from nowhere, and one which she banished just as quickly. A thought that horrified her. If Adam ever found out who she really was he would crucify her, not protect her. Not content with the fact that she'd already served three months in jail, he would do all in his power to punish her even further.

'Penny, what's wrong?'

'Nothing.' She blinked her eyes and tried to pretend she didn't know what he was talking about.

'It doesn't look like nothing to me. You've stabbed that fish a dozen times already. I can assure you it's well and truly dead. What were you thinking?'

There was something fierce in his gaze that made Penny draw in a quick breath. 'It's not important,' she said quietly.

Nostrils flared. 'It is if it makes you look like that. Is it something *I've* done?'

She closed her eyes and shook her head. Hell, why had she fallen in love with the enemy? Why had fate thrust this upon her? And, more importantly, what could she do about it?

It would be so easy to let her guard down. The very thought scared her half to death, but it also served to stiffen her resolve. Why be afraid of someone who didn't even know he was her enemy? Surely she was strong enough to control her panicky feelings during the time he was here?

But you don't know how long he's staying, taunted a spiteful inner voice.

I'll do it for however long it takes, she determined. And once her mind was made up she felt better, and to prove it she finished everything on her plate.

'You're sometimes very difficult to understand.' Adam's dark eyes were pensive on hers as he removed the tray.

'Isn't that a woman's prerogative?'

'I guess it is,' he answered resignedly.

She looked at him, her big green eyes determined. 'I'd like you to leave now, so that I can get some sleep.'

'At this hour?' Adam shot a look at his gold watch. 'It's only half past eight.'

Penny shrugged. 'Nevertheless, I'm tired. So if you wouldn't mind?'

He clearly didn't believe her. He knew it was an excuse to get rid of him, and for a moment he looked as though he wasn't going. He continued to look down at her, to send shock waves through her body, and deliberately she closed her eyes.

She willed him to leave, because she knew that if he didn't, if he remained for much longer, he would end up in her bed. Her body was getting weaker and weaker where Adam Sterne was concerned.

He seemed to stand there for an age before she heard him slowly walk out of the room and the door close with a gentle click. It was only then that Penny realised she had been holding her breath, that her whole body was as rigid as a block of ice.

She had been a fool to say that she would stay. It would be impossible to hide these unbidden feelings, this un-wanted love. It was a dreadful thing that had happened to her. More punishment, in fact. Because there was no way she could ever, ever, allow her love free reign.

Perhaps it wasn't love that she felt. Maybe it was still hatred, manifesting itself in a different form. Didn't they say hatred was akin to love? She was so confused.

Amazingly, though, Penny slept. In fact it was eight o'clock the next morning when she opened her eyes. She was shocked, found it hard to believe that she had slept in so late, and wondered what Lucy Sterne would think when she wasn't there to help her decide what she was going to wear. It had become quite a ritual, going through her wardrobe each morning.

The woman had some lovely clothes, and had told Penny that in her day she'd been a dedicated follower of fashion. 'And I never throw anything away,' she'd added proudly.

It wasn't until she put her foot to the floor that Penny remembered her injured ankle. When she tested it, though, it wasn't quite so painful. She could manage so long as she didn't put too much weight on it.

She ran a shower, but when her thoughts turned to Adam as she was soaping her body, when she wondered what it would be like to have him touch her like this, she deliberately banished them, reminding herself instead of the long, empty days she'd spent in prison, the misery and humiliation she had suffered. It was enough to tighten her lips, and this time there was no doubt that it was hatred filling her heart.

When she limped through to the bedroom after towelling herself dry she found him standing there. To his credit he didn't even bat an eyelid; Penny, on the other hand, was both furious and embarrassed.

Her first instinct was to try and cover herself with her hands, or run back to the bathroom for a towel, or a robe. But something told her he would expect that, so she jutted her chin and forced herself to look at him. 'What are you doing here?'

'I thought you might need help.'

He kept his eyes on hers, although Penny had no doubt that he would have preferred to let them slide over her body. The thought of him looking at her most private parts sensitised every nerve-end.

'The last time I looked in you were fast asleep.'

The cheek of the man, thought Penny fiercely. How dared he keep popping into her room? 'As you can see,' she said tightly, 'I'm managing perfectly well.'

'Is your ankle feeling better?'

'Much better. I don't need any help, thank you. I'll be out for breakfast in just a few minutes.'

He didn't take the hint. He remained standing in exactly the same spot. 'I don't think you should walk on it for a day or two.'

Her eyes flashed a fierce, vivid green. 'I have no intention of making an invalid of myself. And if you must know I strongly object to you invading my privacy.' And if he wasn't going to leave then she'd put her clothes on in front of him. Anything was better than standing here like a fool.

But again she forgot her ankle, and led with her injured foot, wincing loudly as pain shot through it and it almost gave way.

'You damned idiot,' cursed Adam, closing the space in a stride and supporting her with a strong arm. 'Sit down, tell me where your clothes are. I'll help you get dressed.'

'Like hell you will,' returned Penny, ignoring the fire that leapt through her at his touch. 'I can do it myself, thank you very much.' But she allowed him to lead her to the bed so that she could perch on the edge. 'My undies are in that drawer, shorts and T-shirts over there.'

She watched as he selected a pair of delicate lace briefs

and a matching bra, both in white, hating the thought of him seeing these intimate garments, handling them, possibly even imagining putting them on her. An odd twist, she thought wryly. Most men usually dreamt about taking them off.

Cool green shorts were chosen next, and a jade silk top, and finally a pair of flat sandals.

'Yell out when you're ready,' he said lazily, as though what he was doing was the most natural thing in the world. 'And I'll give you an arm to lean on.'

It would have been churlish to refuse, even though that was exactly what she wanted to do, and she nodded, and watched as he left the room.

Actually, and surprisingly, he'd been the perfect gentleman. There was nothing about his behaviour that could offend her. He had not once let his eyes fall from her face, and his touch when her ankle gave way had been perfectly platonic.

She smiled to herself. How often had he touched a naked woman and then been compelled to walk away without taking it any further? Her guess would be never. And probably no other woman would have behaved the way she had. They would have encouraged him, teased him, flaunted themselves a little...

Penny dressed quickly. It was best her thoughts didn't follow this path. It was a deadly dangerous route—not one she had chosen when setting out to destroy Adam Sterne. Her own emotions were not supposed to get involved. So why had they?

It was not a question she could answer, but one that continued to torment her during the days that followed. Adam was far too attentive for her own peace of mind, and she cursed the fact that she'd fallen and sprained her ankle.

One afternoon, when Lucy Sterne was taking her usual

after-lunch nap and Fabian had taken Maggie shopping, the telephone rang. And because Adam was in the pool Penny answered it.

'Hello?' she said. 'The Sterne residence. Can I help you?'

There was a long pause the other end. Then, 'Alex, is that you?'

Penny's heart missed a beat. She recognised the other voice too. The best thing would be to ignore his question and fetch Adam. But already she found herself saying, 'Jon?'

'Good Lord, it *is* you, Alex. What are you doing there?'

What indeed, when Adam Sterne had sacked her from his employ? She sighed heavily. 'It's a long story, Jon, and I'd really rather—'

'Have you gone out of your mind?'

'No, I haven't,' she retorted. 'I'm extremely sane.'

'So answer my question. What are you doing there?'

'I'm Lucy Sterne's companion.'

'And Adam doesn't mind?'

Penny drew in a long unsteady breath. 'He doesn't know who I am.'

'What?'

'I—I've given myself a new identity. And don't you dare tell him.'

'I called round to see you the other day and found your house all locked up. Your neighbour said you'd gone away.'

'You came to see me?' she asked incredulously. 'And yet you never visited me once when I was in jail. God, Jon, what a nerve. Have you any idea how much you hurt me?'

'I had my reasons,' he said quietly.

'I bet you did,' she snapped. 'And I have my reasons for being here. And they don't include talking to you.

Goodbye.' She slammed down the phone before remembering that he was the one who'd made the call and obviously needed to speak to Adam. Oh, well, he could ring again. And this time she most definitely wouldn't answer.

Her heart still thudding, Penny headed for her room. She didn't see Adam standing just inside the doorway, water dripping in a puddle at his feet, black anger darkening his eyes, sitting like thunder on his brow.

A series of images flashed before Adam's mind's eye. The plump and dowdy Alex Brooke, the slender and stylish Penny Brooklyn. The hideous, inelegant Miss Brooke, the graceful, attractive Penny. Long medium-brown hair tied unbecomingly back, corn-blonde hair in a trendy modern style.

Both the same height, yet looking so different. He'd not even noticed the colour of Alexandra Brooke's eyes, and yet he'd immediately seen the spectacular green of Penny Brooklyn's. He would have hated to see Alex Brooke undressed—all that fat. He shuddered. And yet Penny Brooklyn looked fantastic.

How easily he had been taken in. Or had he?

At the interview he'd had a gut feeling that he'd seen her somewhere before. He'd even asked her whether they'd met. What had she answered? 'I'm sure I would remember if we had. You're not the sort of man a woman would easily forget.'

Obviously not. She hadn't forgotten him, would never forget him. She had been out for all she could get then, and, despite her term in jail—or because of it—she was doing the same now. For what other reason was she here? A free three-month holiday, plus whatever perks she could get. Not bad to start with. And then what?

Was she already working on his mother? Was she hoping

for a hand-out either before or after she died? Little did Penny know that Lucy was penniless. His parent didn't even know it herself. Edward had made some very bad investments, as well as spending every last penny on his beloved wife.

He wondered who Penny had been talking to. John, she had called him. Her ex-fiancé, perhaps? And if so how many other times had he rung?

Even as he was thinking this the phone went again, and when he answered it was his technical director. There was a crisis and he was needed back at the office.

Dammit, it couldn't have come at a worse time. He needed to decide what he was going to do about Penny. He didn't want to leave her here with his mother while he went back to England because who knew what she would get up to?

'Did you ring earlier, Jon?' he asked, after confirming that he would catch the first available flight back to England. It was a long shot, but...

'Er, yes, but I thought I had the wrong number.'

Liar, thought Adam. But Jon Byrne—and Penny. Jon and Alex Brooke? He'd had no idea they were connected. It didn't add up. Jon was a smart, intelligent man, good at his job, one of the best. He surely wouldn't jeopardise it by condoning what Alex Brooke had done?

Unless he'd been in it with her?

The thought didn't bear thinking about. And surely he'd heard some rumour that Jon was now engaged to Donna Jackson? What the hell was going on?

Of only one thing was he clear: he was getting rid of Penny Brooklyn once and for all. His mother would have to do without her. Maggie could look after her temporarily until he found someone to take Penny's place.

Heedless of the fact that he was wearing only his wet

swimming shorts, Adam marched along the corridor to Penny's room. His hand raised to push open the door, he suddenly changed his mind.

No, he wouldn't sack her. That was too easy. He'd let her stay on, but he'd be on his guard, he would watch her like a hawk. He would find out exactly what game she was playing, what she was after—and then, at the appropriate moment, he would go in for the kill.

It was very obvious that three months in jail had done nothing to change her. She was still as devious, as cunning, as conniving as she had been when on his design team.

But now she would learn that Adam Sterne was not a man to play around with.

Jon's call disturbed Penny. She'd heard the phone ring again, and the muted sounds of Adam's voice as he answered it. And she was scared to death that Jon would say something. She even waited for Adam to come and throw her out. She even imagined that she heard his footsteps outside her door. But nothing happened and she knew that she was being paranoid.

In fact it was quite a relief to find out from his mother that Adam had suddenly been called back to England. 'Some crisis that only he can deal with,' sniffed Lucy Sterne over dinner. 'I expect it's the last we'll see of him. It was such a surprise him coming out here. I have to be honest, Penny, I thought it was because of you.'

'Me?' Penny's eyes opened wide. 'You mean he came to check up on me?'

'Of course not, my dear. I thought he was—at least I hoped he was—attracted to you. I'm a silly old woman, I know, but I think you two would be eminently suited.'

A flush crept through Penny's cheeks as she shook her head repeatedly. 'I appreciate the thought, Mrs Sterne, but

I'm not interested in your son, not in that way.' She spoke very firmly, because Lord help her if his mother ever found out that she'd fallen in love with him.

The woman grimaced wryly. 'That's a pity. Does Adam know?'

Surely his mother hadn't seen what was going on between them, thought Penny in surprise. Nevertheless, she admitted reluctantly, 'I guess he does.' He'd be a fool if he didn't, after the way she'd treated him.

'Does that mean—he did show an interest and you turned him down?' There was an eager light now in Lucy Sterne's pale blue eyes.

Penny groaned. Why hadn't she kept her mouth shut? 'I don't think,' she said slowly, 'that this is the sort of conversation you and I should be having.'

'Why don't you like my son?'

Yet another direct question! She winced inwardly. 'It's not that I don't like him,' she replied quietly. 'He's—he's quite a guy. I guess I'm not interested in any man at the moment.'

Lucy frowned. 'Is there a reason? You're such an attractive girl that—'

'My fiancé ditched me a few months ago—at the same time as I lost my job.'

'Ah!' The older woman nodded understandingly. 'And now you're anti-men. But, my dear, they're not all the same. Adam would never do that to anyone. He has the kindest heart imaginable. He would never get engaged unless he was absolutely sure that she was the right woman. He has yet to find her. I'd like to think it could be you.'

'But, Mrs Sterne—' Penny knew she had to stop Adam's mother '—he's already in love with someone else.'

Lucy frowned. 'What are you talking about? If Adam

had a girlfriend I'd most certainly know about it. Did he tell you this?'

Penny nodded.

'Who is she?'

'I don't know. I did get the impression, though, that his feelings weren't returned.'

'There you are, then,' said his mother triumphantly. 'What point would there be in him going after someone who doesn't love him? None at all. So you may as well forget what he said.'

'It really doesn't matter to me,' said Penny.

'Don't you like him just a little bit?'

Penny couldn't help laughing. 'Mrs Sterne, you can't make us fall in love. I can understand you wanting to see your son settled, but it won't be with me.'

The woman looked at her long and hard. 'Did you two have a row?'

'What do you mean, a row? When?' Penny tried to stall for time, even though she knew exactly what Adam's mother was talking about.

'When you went on your walk the other day. Adam's been very distracted since.'

'Probably because of my ankle,' ventured Penny.

'And probably not,' snorted the older woman. 'I'm not blind. I can see what's going on.' Then she heaved a sigh. 'The next few days will tell me whether or not he's interested.'

Warily Penny looked at her. 'What do you mean?'

'If he comes back, it will definitely be because of you. He only came once when Edward and I used to stay here. He always said he was too busy.'

'It was probably because you had each other,' Penny said quickly. 'Now, because you're on your own, it's only natural he'd want to make sure you're all right.'

'So why did he hire you?' returned the older woman smartly. 'He always says he can't afford to take time off. So you explain to me why he suddenly managed it this time.'

Penny shrugged and spread her hands wide. 'I haven't the faintest idea.'

'Such innocence,' said Mrs Sterne. 'Really, Penny, you should open your eyes.'

Penny chewed her lower lip. She did not like Adam's mother's fixation.

'Why don't we have a little bet?' said Lucy, suddenly and slyly. 'If Adam doesn't come back then I'll accept that he has no interest in you and I'll humbly apologise. But if he does I'd like you to forget your prejudices and—allow him to get a little closer.'

'Mrs Sterne!' Green eyes widened in protest.

'You have to get on with your life. You can't let what one man did ruin it for ever.'

'But—'

'But nothing, my dear. Let's just wait and see what happens.'

And so they did.

And two days later Adam returned.

CHAPTER SEVEN

As ADAM drove the last leg of his journey to the Villa Mimosa his resolve to catch Penny Brooklyn out was as strong as ever. She was a devious, cunning woman, and he fully intended making sure that she got everything she deserved.

He'd spoken to Jon Byrne over a social drink, and through careful questioning had found to his relief that Jon had had nothing to do with Alex Brooke's crime.

'I still find it hard to believe that Alex did it,' Jon had said with a faint shake of his head. 'I never thought she was the type. In fact I'd have bet my life she wasn't. It just goes to show.'

Adam sipped his whisky and nodded as though in agreement. 'You were once engaged, I believe?'

'It was something we drifted into,' admitted Jon with a rueful smile, and he looked faintly surprised that Adam knew this. 'Something Alex wanted more than I did, as a matter of fact. And to be quite frank I'd been after a way of ending it for quite a while.'

'Because you were having an affair with Donna Jackson?'

Jon almost choked on his beer. 'I wasn't aware it was common knowledge.'

'Is anything ever secret in a place the size of Sterne?' Adam wanted to know. 'And now I understand you're engaged to her?' He'd been making various enquiries since his return and found out a whole lot of things he hadn't known before—should have known, really. In future he would make it his business to know as much about his employees as he did about the work they did.

Another grimace from Jon and a faint nod.

He actually looked guilty, thought Adam.

'Donna had been on to me for ages to tell Alex,' he admitted. 'To tell you the truth she used to get quite angry about it. But I didn't want to hurt Alex's feelings. We'd known each other for so long that I felt I should let her down gently.'

'You must have been pleased when the opportunity presented itself?' Mention of Donna's anger interested Adam. He'd heard a few things about Donna Jackson that were worth further investigation.

'I wasn't pleased for you, or the company,' Jon said quickly, urgently, 'but, well, yes, it did let me off the hook—though not exactly in a way I would have chosen.'

'You do know, of course, that she's working for me again?'

'Er—well…'

'It's all right, Jon. I know you spoke to her the other day. I actually overheard some of the conversation.' His mouth tightened as he recalled that revealing moment. 'I didn't know until then who she was. She'd fooled me completely. She's calling herself Penny Brooklyn these days.'

'Penny's her middle name,' Jon informed him.

'Is that so? Well, she's totally transformed the way she looks. She's slim and svelte and absolutely stunning. Even a different hairstyle and colour. You wouldn't recognise her.'

'She did say something on the phone about changing her identity,' Jon admitted. 'But I didn't know she'd gone that far. As long as I've known her she's always carried a little extra weight, and always worn her hair the same.' He shook his head, as if trying to assimilate this new image of the girl he'd once loved.

'What I find difficult to understand,' he added after a moment's pause, a frown of concentration on his face, 'is why she'd want to work for you again. I'd have thought she'd be frightened to death of coming anywhere near you after what she—after what happened.'

Adam nodded his agreement. 'Who knows the way her mind works?' He could have told Jon that he suspected she was up to her tricks again, but there was just a chance that Jon, with a pang of conscience for old times' sake, might tell Penny that Adam had discovered her identity, and that was a risk he didn't dare take.

But now, as he neared the house, he found himself wondering why he hadn't got rid of her straight away. It would have been by far the easiest solution. Better than spending time he could ill afford watching and waiting.

Penny and Lucy Sterne were in the middle of lunch when Adam arrived. His mother, as usual, was highly delighted to see him. 'Adam, how lovely. I wasn't sure you'd find the time to come back.' And there was wicked triumph in her pale eyes as she looked at Penny.

'Adam,' Penny acknowledged quietly.

'How's your ankle?' he asked in return.

'Good. Almost better.' Lord, it was good to see him. He looked absolutely dynamic, so alive, so vital, and certainly not as though he'd spent the last twelve hours or more travelling.

'I'm glad to hear it.' He didn't smile as he looked at her. In fact his tone was almost terse.

'Sit down and join us,' fussed his mother.

But Adam shook his head. 'I'm not hungry. What I need more than anything is a shower. If you'll excuse me?'

The air, which had gone thick and heavy while he stood there, suddenly thinned, allowing Penny to breathe again. She hadn't realised until he'd turned up exactly how much she had missed him, how empty the villa had felt without him.

'Don't forget our bet,' said his mother in an exaggerated whisper.

'I think that rather depends on Adam,' Penny returned sharply. She'd hoped the woman would forget the silly bet.

'Nonsense!' Lucy returned. 'I might be old, but I do know that times have changed, that girls very often make the first move. You can't let me down now, Penny, I won't let you.'

Penny didn't argue, but how could she do as his mother wanted? Especially as she had repeatedly rejected him. Besides, she wasn't here for that reason. It was Adam's downfall she wanted, not his love.

It occurred to her that she hadn't yet found a way of bringing that about. She hadn't asked his mother enough about him, hadn't discovered his weaknesses—if he had any! The more she saw of him the more she was inclined to believe that Adam was omnipotent. That nothing could harm him. That no matter how she tried he would always come out the victor.

As usual, Lucy Sterne retired to her room after lunch, but not before she had given Penny a huge wink. Get on with it, girl, she seemed to be saying. She really was a remarkable old lady, thought Penny. Nothing like Adam had described her. Irascible and querulous, he had said. Instead she had found her warm and humorous and a joy to be with.

Penny knew that the best thing she could do now was keep out of Adam's way. She didn't believe for one minute that he was back because of her. It was what his mother wanted to believe, but it had to be far from the truth.

So why was he here?

To keep an eye on his mother? To make sure Penny was doing her job properly? Because he needed a holiday? It could be none of them, or it could be all three. Or it could be something different altogether.

So deep in thought was she as she headed for her room that she didn't see Adam until she bumped into him, until his arms reached out to steady her.

And when she looked up, an apology on her lips, he seemed to be looking at her and yet not seeing her. It was an odd sensation, causing her stomach muscles to tighten and a sense of unease to run through her body. Fingers crossed Jon had said nothing.

'Is something on your mind?'

Shaking her head, Penny tried to pull away, but his hands remained firm on her upper arms.

'I was going to fetch a magazine,' she said. 'I thought I'd sit outside.'

'And that required a lot of concentration, did it?'

There was something very different about him, thought Penny. He'd either found out who she was, or he was still worried about whatever had taken him back to England. She hoped it was the latter. 'Did you sort things out?' she asked, instead of answering his question.

A frown creased his forehead. 'What do you mean?'

'Your mother said there was a problem no one else could handle.'

'Oh, that, yes. All's well now. Jon Byrne, my technical director, could have dealt with it himself, as a matter of fact. But I'm glad he sent for me. There was something else we needed to discuss.'

His eyes never left her face, cool, assessing, with an odd glitter that she had never seen before.

He did know!

More unease quivered through her body. But, no, he couldn't. Jon wouldn't have said anything, would he? Not when she'd told him not to.

On the other hand she'd never thought he would dump her in her hour of need. It proved that you never really knew a person, no matter how close you were, how long you had known them.

'Forget the magazine,' Adam was saying now. 'Come and join me instead. Tell me how much you've missed me.' And, taking her hand, he pulled her along with him.

'You look troubled,' he said once they were seated on a shady part of the terrace, long, ice-cold drinks in front of them. 'Has my mother been playing up?'

Penny sat stiffly, her hands clenched in her lap, intensely conscious of him beside her, of the way her hormones played havoc at his nearness. The truth was she *had* missed him. And now he was back she was afraid of letting down her defences.

'Your mother never plays up,' she told him. 'I get on very well with her.'

A faint frown, gone in an instant. She might have imagined it. 'She seems to have taken quite a liking to you.'

'As I have to her,' said Penny.

'It's good that you get on so well.'

She eyed him with a questioning lift of one fine brow. 'I don't imagine you'd have chosen me for the job if you hadn't thought we would.'

'That's true,' he admitted with a wry twist of his lips. 'But my mother can be extremely difficult.'

'She's never been anything but kind to me,' she told him,

adding sharply, 'If you're back to check whether I'm doing my job properly, then I can assure you—'

'That's not why I'm here, Penny.'

She felt sick to the pit of her stomach. But she betrayed none of her unease. 'Your mother wasn't sure you'd return. She says it's most unlike you.'

'Then perhaps there's another reason.'

His voice had deepened, and Penny read desire in his velvet dark eyes, desire he was doing nothing to hide.

It was an instant change of mood. It took her completely by surprise. It also sent shivers of awareness over her skin. It made her gasp, it made her forget that a second ago he'd looked at her with suspicion, and it made her forget also that he was her enemy and her main aim was to destroy him.

'I—er—what is that?'

'I think you know.'

'No, I don't,' she said huskily, wishing she understood this change in him.

'Oh, come on, Penny. You're not that blind.'

'No, I'm not,' she agreed, realising the pointlessness of pretending she didn't know what he was talking about. 'But I've already told you. I don't want any kind of relationship.'

She tried to ignore the warmth of her senses, the liquid desire that began to pump through her body. Why was he doing this? A few seconds ago he'd looked at her so coldly, so condemningly, and yet now...

'I think we agreed on friendship,' he said.

'You're not looking at me like a friend.'

A dark brow quirked. 'Is that so?'

'You're looking at me as though you want to take me to bed.'

'Maybe I do.'

Penny closed her eyes briefly in a vain attempt to squash her wilful feelings. 'This is ridiculous,' she said firmly. And the last thing she had expected.

'I can't see what's ridiculous about two people wanting each other.'

It was amazing how that one word hurt. *Want!* He wanted her, full stop. He didn't love her as she had discovered she loved him, he would never love her, he simply wanted to feed his hungry body. Maybe he *had* found out who she was and this was *his* form of revenge. Well, he could go on wanting. He could want for the rest of his life.

Penny sprang to her feet. 'If you think that I would ever, *ever* let you make love to me, you must be raving mad. You're the last man on earth I'd let do that.'

Her legs were trembling as she walked away, her face flaming. She was both furious and embarrassed. And to add insult to injury she saw Lucy Sterne watching them from her bedroom window.

'Penny.' Adam followed her into the house.

'What?' She turned and faced him coldly.

'What's this all about?'

She shook her head. 'I don't know what you mean.'

'Oh, I think you do. I think the truth is you're afraid to show your feelings. In fact, Miss Penny Brooklyn, I think you might even feel guilty that you're beginning to get over the loss of your fiancé.'

Penny's eyes flashed their usual vivid green. 'Why should I feel guilty?'

'You tell me.'

She shook her head. 'You're crazy. You don't know what you're talking about.'

'So why are you freezing me out when we both know there's a mutual attraction?'

'Mutual?' she echoed scathingly. 'I don't think so. What

are you saying? That you fancy me, that you want an affair? Is that why you've come back?'

Her outspokenness seemed to surprise him. His brows rose; his thickly lashed eyes widened. 'Actually, having an affair with you was the last thing on my mind,' he told her bluntly.

'Then what the hell are you playing at?' she wanted to know, ignoring her thudding senses, putting them down to anger rather than desire.

'I'm not *playing* at anything,' he retorted. 'My body's reaction is a perfectly natural one. It's not something I planned. You're a hell of a sexy lady. Didn't you know that?'

Penny cursed the flush that stole over her cheeks. 'I'm flattered that you should think so. But I'm not into playing those kind of games.'

'What games do you play, then?' There was a subtle change in him, a stillness, a faint thinning of his lips. Penny wouldn't have noticed if she hadn't been watching him; there was no change in his voice, in fact he even smiled. And yet...

You're being paranoid, she told herself. You're imagining things. You feel guilty because you're here under false pretences. 'I don't play games of any sort,' she snapped. 'I've had enough of this conversation. I'm going to my room.'

But again he stopped her. And this time he took her arm and turned her to face him, and he didn't let go. Penny's quickened heartbeats echoed in her ears and she wanted to close her eyes, to shut him out, to ignore him completely.

Impossible.

She could almost hear the throb of his heart too, and when he pulled her against him she felt the shocking hardness of his manhood. She did close her eyes then, not want-

ing to look into those pools of velvet brown in case she
sank and became helpless.

Why was he doing this? What was he trying to prove?
What was he hoping to gain?

When his mouth came down on hers she gave a mew of
protest, which was ignored, and she pressed her hands
against his strongly muscled chest, but to no avail.

Adam's hands slid behind her back; they held, they imprisoned, and they totally destroyed. There was no way now
that she could resist him.

Her lips parted involuntarily, they allowed his tongue
entrance, and the sweet headiness of his kiss sent a thousand different sensations reverberating through every corner of her body.

Of their own volition her hands moved over the solid
muscle of his shoulders, and the heady scent of him invaded
her nostrils, adding to and increasing the desire building
inside her.

It was madness, it was insanity, it went against her every
instinct, but some driving force would not let her call a
halt. The taste of him was like a drug, and she knew it
would remain with her for ever, long after they'd parted
company, long after he'd forgotten her.

She accepted his kiss with an eagerness that should have
disturbed her, should have made her ashamed. Instead she
pressed her body into the heated urgency of his with little
regard for the consequences.

He seemed to be drawing a response from her without
even trying, taking what only a few seconds ago she had
been unprepared to give.

Her heart slammed hard now against her ribcage, an impossible heat building up as her mouth moved with fierce
passion over his. And when his hand moved to gently cup
the mound of her breast, thumb brushing her already hard-

ened nipple with tantalising slowness, she wanted to cry out her pleasure.

She wanted to rip off her cotton top, her lacy slip of a bra, and give his hand free reign. She wanted to feel his skin against hers, his hard hands against her delicate softness, to see the tanned colour of his skin against her much paler one.

She wanted to hold him against her, arch her body in supplication, offer herself to him.

All these thoughts flashed through her mind, and just as quickly were followed by stone-cold reasoning. What was she doing? Didn't she realise where it would end? Didn't she know what sort of an interpretation he might put on her acquiescence?

'Adam, no!' The words were forced through her lips, but instead of being strong and meaningful her voice was low and hesitant, pleading almost. And Adam wasn't the sort of man you could plead with.

He continued his agonising assault as though she hadn't spoken. His lips continued to tantalise, to draw out from the depth of her soul feelings she had not known she possessed.

Kissing Jon had never been like this. It had been—ordinary. That was the word that sprang to mind. Ordinary. Pleasant, yes, giving rise to pleasant feelings that she'd thought were the most anyone ever felt when they were in love.

But it had been nothing as mind-blowing as Adam's kiss now, and he wasn't even trying! She could sense that he was holding back, that he was playing with her, teasing her, wanting to see how far she would let him go.

She had been so firm in her rejection of him, telling him only a few short minutes ago that he was the last man on earth she would let make love to her.

So where was that resolve? What was happening to her? Why wasn't she in control? Damn, and damn again. This was all wrong. This wasn't in her plan of things at all.

Again she spoke. 'Adam, please…'

'Please what?' He spoke against her mouth, his breath warm and fresh—and essentially Adam. Though what made her think that she didn't know. Essentially Adam. What did that mean? 'Please, you want more?' A thumb and forefinger squeezed her taut nipple, creating further shock waves, further revealing sensations.

Slow inch by slow inch he was breaking down her defences, infiltrating her barriers, and soon—if she did not put a stop to it—he would ride triumphant over every last crumbling rock. He would take, he would penetrate, he would master.

All in the name of want.

Not love.

Never love.

Want.

Animal hunger.

Male domination.

'Damn you, Adam Sterne.' Her voice was strong now, firm and resolute. 'You cannot do this to me. Stop! *Stop now!*' She beat her fists against his chest, her darkened green eyes glittering and furious.

He smiled.

Damn him, he smiled!

'I wondered how far you'd let me go,' he said lazily.

'If you were a gentleman you'd have stopped when I first asked you.'

His infuriating smile widened. 'Even that was much further into the proceedings than I'd imagined.'

'Proceedings?' she spat. 'Proceedings? What the devil kind of man are you?'

'I'm a very human one,' he told her.

'You could have fooled me.'

'And you're a very exciting lady.'

'Really?' She looked at him coldly now. 'Someone to play games with, is that what you're saying? Someone with whom to while away a few hours while you're here for God knows what purpose? The pleasure might be yours, but it's certainly not mine.'

He cocked his head to one side and studied her thoughtfully. 'You experienced no pleasure at all?'

He would know she was lying if she said no, so Penny shrugged. 'It all depends what one calls pleasure,' she returned coolly. 'Being kissed by a man who already knows I want nothing to do with him is tantamount to an attack as far as I'm concerned.'

She was going over the top, she knew, but, Lord, he was making her mad.

A dark flush stole over his skin, but he controlled his temper far better than she was able. 'I'm sure you don't mean that, Penny.'

'You'll never know whether I do or not,' she said smartly, and, turning on her heel, she strode swiftly away. And this time he let her go.

Penny shut herself in her room with every intention of staying there for the rest of the day. This was awful. This was something she hadn't anticipated. Despite the love she felt for him, she'd been sure that she had the strength to ignore it, to fend off any advances.

It was quite a shock discovering how easily she'd capitulated. And it made her realise how dangerous it was to let Adam anywhere near. Yet how could she avoid it? His mother spent so much time in her room that it was only natural they'd be thrust together.

Again she wondered why he was here. She knew the

interpretation Lucy Sterne had put on her son returning, but she refused to believe it. It was too ridiculous for words.

Adam here because of her! No! She shook her head vigorously. It was out of the question. He was by far too conscientious a man to turn his back on work for the sake of an affair.

Still shaking her head, Penny moved through to the bathroom, peeling off her shorts and shirt before stepping beneath the cool jets of the shower. Her intention was to wash Adam out of her hair, as the song said, but it wasn't that easy.

Adam refused to go away. His hand still stroked her breast, his mouth still captured and tormented, and every nerve-end in her body remained sensitised.

How could she escape this madness without letting Lucy Sterne down? Why didn't Adam go away, never to return? How long was he going to stay? Not for the whole three months, please God. Not even for another week. If he did he would destroy her.

Impatiently she turned the shower off, tugged on her towelling robe and threw herself down on the bed. Almost immediately she heard a tap on the door.

'Go away,' she called out. 'I don't want to speak to you.' She ought to have locked it. She might have known he would come after her again.

'It's me, Penny.'

Oh, hell! His mother! And she'd told her to go away! She should have realised it wasn't Adam. He'd have thumped on the door, not tapped, and he wouldn't have stood and waited, he'd have waltzed right in.

She sprang to her feet and ran lightly across the room. 'I'm sorry,' she said as she opened the door.

'You thought I was Adam?' asked Lucy Sterne, a wry smile on her lips.

'Yes, Mrs Sterne, I'm afraid I did. I'm so sorry I spoke to you like that.'

'Don't fret, my dear. May I come in?'

'Of course.' Penny stood back, and the older woman's walking stick tapped rhythmically on the tiles as she made her way to the chair near the window.

'I have an apology to make myself,' said Lucy Sterne.

A faint frown tugged Penny's fine brows together. 'You do?' She couldn't think what it might be.

'I'm afraid I eavesdropped on you and Adam.'

'Oh!' Penny's hand involuntarily came to her mouth, and her luminous green eyes widened.

'I know it was wrong of me, but I saw you storm away from him by the pool so I set out to intercept you. I wanted to talk, to find out what had gone wrong. I know it's none of my business, but I'm an old woman and I don't want to see all my hopes crumbling into ashes at my feet.'

'Mrs Sterne, you cannot force things to happen,' said Penny gently.

'I know, my dear,' she replied on a trembling sigh. 'But it would make me so happy. I'm quite sure my son's not playing games with you. He wouldn't do that. He's serious, I'm certain.'

Penny pulled her lips down at the corners and shook her head lightly. 'I'm sorry, I can't agree with you.'

'I think you're not giving him a chance,' said Lucy sadly. 'You did promise me, you know.' There was a reproving look in the pale blue eyes, and a twisting of bony fingers on her lap.

'I promised nothing,' Penny declared firmly.

'Have you forgotten our bet?'

How could she forget it? Such a stupid thing. 'We didn't shake on it,' she pointed out firmly.

Lucy Sterne smiled. 'But neither did you say that you

wouldn't let him get closer. I thought for one moment when he kissed you that... Oh, dear.' It was the older woman's turn to clap her hand to her mouth. 'I've given myself away, haven't I?'

Penny's cheeks were almost blood-red.

Lucy chuckled. 'Oh, well, now you know that I was unashamedly watching you.' She didn't look in the least embarrassed.

'You reminded me of me and Edward when we first met. I fought my attraction to him like the very devil because, like you, I'd decided he was only playing with me. It turned out he wasn't. He loved me very much, but he wasn't a man who could easily declare his feelings. He thought if he showed them I'd understand how he felt.'

'And you think that's what Adam's doing?' asked Penny drily. Personally she doubted it. Adam wasn't shy; he was never at a loss for words. Far from it. If he loved someone he'd tell them.

'Naturally, I can't say for certain,' said Lucy, 'but, Penny, I'm his mother. I know he wouldn't be here if it wasn't for you.'

He could be here because he knows who I am!

Penny immediately dismissed the thought. If he knew then he sure as hell wouldn't keep quiet about it. He would sack her instantly. He wouldn't give her space in his house. And he most certainly wouldn't want to make love to her.

'I'm sorry I can't agree with you,' she said quietly, sadly. She felt sorry for Lucy, who was fighting for her own happiness, but surely the woman could see that nothing she said would make any difference. She couldn't run her son's life for him.

And what would Adam say if he knew his mother was

here now, pleading on his behalf? He would be furious, Penny was sure.

Even as she was thinking this the door burst open and Adam came storming in.

CHAPTER EIGHT

ADAM pulled up short when he saw his mother in Penny's room. What the hell was she doing here? He'd intended questioning Penny, but with his mother present what excuse could he give for barging in?

He'd been unable to help himself when he kissed her. Even knowing the reason she was here on this island had made no difference. She'd got beneath his skin like no other woman ever had.

Where he'd expected the kiss to lead he didn't know— but he certainly hadn't expected her to be quite so strongly offensive about it. Her rejection confused him. It didn't make sense.

To his surprise, though, his mother didn't seem to see anything wrong in his appearance. She simply smiled, a mysterious smile he couldn't quite understand, and then announced that she was leaving.

'It's very obvious, Adam, that you have something you wish to say to Penny,' she said. 'I'll leave you to get on with it.' Tap, tap went her stick as she made her way out, echoing the strong beat of his heart as he stood and waited.

The second the door closed, before he had a chance to speak, Penny turned on him. 'What the devil do you want? If you think you can kiss me again you're deeply mistaken.'

Her lovely green eyes were stormy, the lines of her body spelt resistance, and yet still he felt an immense attraction. It annoyed him as much as it disturbed and excited him. What the hell was wrong with him that he should feel this way for a common criminal?

The truth was she didn't look like a criminal. She looked as honest as the day was long. Even that day she'd come to his office pleading her innocence there'd been a part of him that had wanted to believe her. And yet all the proof had been put before him. He'd had no choice but to dismiss her and inform the police.

'I want an apology,' he said in answer to her question. It wasn't something he'd planned to say, and it would get him nowhere, but it seemed appropriate in the face of such hostility.

'For what?' she demanded to know, tightening the belt of her towelling robe as she glared at him, straightening her back, jutting her chin.

Guessing she was naked beneath, Adam felt his desire surge, and he wanted more than anything to slide his hands inside and feel the soft warmth of her skin, inhale the sweet, heady fragrance of her, urge her hard against him—*make her his!*

This last thought sent shock waves through his body, ripple after ripple after ripple, every instinct, every urge intensified. He really would have to be careful. 'You should know what I'm talking about. For declaring that I attacked you.'

Her chin lifted even higher, her cheeks flamed, her eyes flashed brilliant sparks of danger. And, Lord, how beautiful it made her look.

'I said it was *tantamount* to an attack,' she pointed out icily, her whole body rejecting him. 'Not the same thing at all.'

'Nevertheless you were insinuating that I took without asking.'

'And didn't you?' She again pulled at the ties of her robe, as if aware of her vulnerability, as if she had to make very, very certain that nothing was exposed to him, not one inch of flesh—in case it tantalised him further, and…

He shoved clenched fists into his pockets. He wasn't used to women thinking this way about him. It made him feel like a monster instead of a gentleman—which he had always prided himself on being.

'No, I don't think I did,' he said with quiet dignity. 'And if you look deep inside yourself you'll know it's the truth.'

'I've already looked deep,' she told him cruelly. 'And I haven't changed my mind, not one iota. What you did is unforgivable.'

'Except that *you* kissed me as though you really wanted to,' he thrust back. Dammit, he wasn't going to let her get away with making him feel the guilty one. He'd done nothing to be ashamed of.

'Haven't you ever stopped to think that maybe I was just curious?'

'Curious?' This had to be the worst reason he'd heard for wanting to kiss someone. 'And did I satisfy that curiosity?'

Penny eyed him disdainfully. 'I refuse to answer. And if you wouldn't mind I'd like to get dressed.' She walked to the door and yanked it open—but Adam was not yet ready to go.

Calmly he removed her hand and closed it again. 'I'd like to know what my mother was doing here.' But the fact that she was now standing ruinously close, that he could smell the spring freshness of her shower gel, that he could see a tantalising glimpse of gorgeous breast through the vee of her robe—which she quickly bunched into her fist as she saw his eyes drop—made his question seem unimportant.

He wanted only to hold her. Dammit, it was insane, but the need rose in him and he knew that he ought to leave, that to remain here was the most dangerous thing he'd ever done.

This woman—whom he'd thought he despised, thought he distrusted, *ought* to distrust—had got through to him like no one else ever had.

'I think that's my business.' She threw him a look that suggested he had no right even asking the question.

'Did you invite her?' Did they get together often like this? Was Penny wooing his mother? Was she getting her on side, doing all in her power to get her hands on what she thought was Lucy Sterne's wealth?

The thought that Penny could be plotting and planning for her future brought him to his senses, and he looked at her sternly, relieved that some of his intense desire was fading, that he could face her without his heart pounding, without lusty thoughts savaging him.

'No, I didn't,' she answered, her green eyes level on his.

'So why did she come?'

'She wanted to talk to me.'

'About what?' What could his mother have to say that wouldn't wait?

'I think that's between me and your mother,' she said, but faint colour rose in her throat and spread to her cheeks, and he knew without a shadow of doubt that she had something to hide.

'Dammit, Penny, I demand that you tell me.' Of course he knew that she wouldn't, that she would go to any lengths to hide what she was plotting, but fury was now building where desire had once been, and he felt like shaking her, not letting her go until she told him.

'You cannot force me to do anything.' Chin stubborn, eyes glittering, she swung away from him.

But Adam wasn't allowing that. He put a firm hand on

her shoulder and spun her to face him—and as he did so her belt came tumbling undone!

It was more than flesh and blood could stand. A tempting glimpse of softly rounded curves, of flat stomach and a triangle of shadow, sent fresh desire rampaging through him.

All the feelings he had clamped down on came rushing back to the surface, and with a stifled groan, with a shake of his head, he yanked open the door he had only seconds ago closed, and let himself out.

When he reached his own room he found he was trembling. How could one woman—and this woman in particular—have such a devastating effect on him? Somehow he had to feed his anger, stoke it to boiling point, not let this need, this deep desire, take such a hold.

And the only way to do it was to constantly remind himself of what she'd done. She had stolen a design, a highly secret design, for a revolutionary new type of alarm system—and now his competitors were set to make a fortune from it.

This was what he needed to think about, this and nothing else, and when he joined Penny and his mother for dinner his face was rigid with anger.

'Is something wrong, dear?' asked his mother as Maggie served a delicious-looking seafood salad.

'No.'

'You look a little—upset.'

'No, I'm not.'

'That's all right, then,' she said. 'Because I want to ask you a favour.'

'By all means.' He answered her almost absently, looking instead at Penny, who was wearing a flattering blue cotton dress with a scooped neckline and a short flared skirt. But he wasn't seeing the dress, he was seeing instead her perfectly formed body beneath, and he felt a stirring in his groin that belied every effort he'd made to rid his mind of such feelings.

'I want you to take Penny sailing tomorrow,' announced his mother with a pleased smile.

'What?' He jerked his head back towards his parent, but not before he'd seen Penny's equally shocked expression. 'Why?'

'Why? Do you have to ask that question? Because I think she'd enjoy it. Edward and I used to go sailing. It's an experience no one should miss.'

'We no longer have the boat, Mother. We sold it when Father died, if you remember.' Spending a whole day alone with Penny was the last thing he wanted. Under different circumstances, if she'd been a different person, it would have been perfect, he would probably have suggested it himself, but as things stood...

'Then hire one,' Lucy Sterne told him impatiently. 'Heavens, Adam, anyone would think you didn't want to take Penny.'

He speared a prawn and tossed it into his mouth, swallowing it without tasting and then prodding another, unaware of his mother watching closely for his reaction. 'Have you thought that Penny might not want to go?' he asked, knowing he sounded grumpy—but how dared his mother put him into this situation?

'Penny?' Lucy turned her attention to her young companion. 'For heaven's sake, tell my son that you'd love a day at sea.'

'Actually, Mrs Sterne,' said Penny, 'I wouldn't. I get very seasick. I wouldn't enjoy it at all.'

Adam's relief knew no bounds.

'I have some pills that will soon put a stop to that,' announced the older woman firmly.

But Penny still shook her head. 'I'd really rather not, if you don't mind.'

The woman shook her head as she looked from one to the other. 'I'm sure I don't know what's wrong with you two. I thought it would be a perfect day.'

'I appreciate you thinking about us,' said Penny, and she sounded guilty for turning his mother's offer down.

And maybe she was, he thought. Maybe she didn't want to do anything that would make her lose favour. But thank goodness she suffered from seasickness. It had certainly let him off the hook.

He tried to imagine what it would have been like. The two of them constantly skirting around each other, sexual tension in the air. And he wouldn't have dared touch her or she'd have pushed him overboard. It would have been a hellish day.

Perhaps he ought to return to England. Perhaps it had been a big mistake coming back. She couldn't do anything while she was here except worm her way into his mother's affections, and that wouldn't get her very far—not on a monetary level anyway. And once they were home he'd make very sure that she had no further part to play in their lives.

Conversation was stilted for the rest of the meal. Lucy continued to look hurt, and Penny tried her very best to be cheerful, but there was a definite atmosphere, and as soon as he could decently manage it Adam excused himself.

He took the car and drove hard into Castries, where he went to his favourite bar and spent the night drinking. And then, foolishly, he decided to drive home! It was unlike him to take such a risk, but Penny Brooklyn, or Alex Brooke, or whatever she wanted to call herself, had got him into such a state that at times he didn't know what he was doing.

To his alarm, to his consternation, when he got there all the lights were on in the villa and an ambulance stood outside.

'Do you really suffer from seasickness, Penny, or was that an excuse not to spend time with Adam?'

The two women were still sitting at the table, long after Adam had gone. They'd talked about all sorts of things: they'd discussed tastes in music, in books, in films, and they'd virtually put the world to rights, but now Lucy Sterne brought the conversation round to her son, as Penny had guessed she would.

'Yes, I do,' she said. 'I really do.'

'But not so badly that a couple of pills wouldn't cure it?' Lucy asked astutely.

'I guess so,' Penny admitted, knowing exactly what was in Adam's mother's mind.

The woman was quiet for a moment, then she said, 'I know it's none of my business, but did you and Adam have a row after I left your room? Is that why you don't want to spend time together?'

Penny lifted her shoulders and pulled a guilty face. 'We did have words. He wanted to know what you were doing there and I wouldn't tell him.'

Lucy's thin brows rose and her pale eyes gleamed. 'Did he indeed? But surely that proves my point. My son's definitely interested in you.'

'Is that why he jumped at the excuse *not* to take me sailing?' Penny's voice was loaded with sarcasm.

'You know what I mean,' said the older woman with some asperity. 'He can't keep away from you. He has to know everything you're doing or saying.' Then she smiled warmly. 'Believe me, my dear, I know exactly the way his mind works.'

'I wish I could say the same,' said Penny, fiddling with the spoon in her saucer. And, in a desperate attempt to close the subject, 'I could do with another cup of coffee. Would you like one?'

'No, thank you. I think I'll go to my room. Perhaps Adam will feel better when he comes back.'

Penny doubted it. She doubted there would ever be peace between her and this woman's son.

With her attention on the coffee she was pouring, Penny didn't actually see what happened next. All she heard was a thud and an alarmed cry as Lucy Sterne landed heavily on the floor.

'Mrs Sterne.' She was on her feet immediately, crouching over the older woman. 'Oh, Mrs Sterne.' She could see by the way her leg was sticking out at a grotesque angle that she had broken her hip. 'Don't try to move. I'll send for an ambulance. Are you in a lot of pain?'

The woman grimaced. 'Some.'

But she wouldn't complain, Penny knew; Lucy Sterne was a tough old lady. She ran to find Maggie, and asked her to make the call, then she raced back to Lucy and put a cushion beneath her head and a blanket over her.

'Where's Adam?' demanded the older woman.

'I think he went out,' Penny told her. 'I heard his car earlier.'

'Damned boy, never here when I want him.'

'I'll check whether he's back.' But she found his car still missing and his room empty. 'I'm sorry,' she said, touching Lucy's arm sympathetically. 'I'm sure he won't be long.'

His mother snorted disbelievingly. 'He wasn't in a very good mood. He's probably drowning his sorrows in drink somewhere.'

Penny frowned. 'He wouldn't do that, would he?' Adam

had never struck her as the type to resort to drink when things went wrong.

'Who knows what he'll do?'

Penny felt guilty now that she had quarrelled with him. If she hadn't he would be here, when his mother needed him. If she hadn't this whole thing might never have happened!

Maggie came bustling in to say that the ambulance would be here shortly, and kept asking whether there was anything she could do, anything she could get, until finally Lucy sent her away.

'I can't stand fuss,' she said to Penny. 'I just wish Adam was here, that's all.'

But Adam hadn't returned by the time the ambulance arrived, and Mrs Sterne began to look more and more agitated. 'Where is he?' she asked tetchily of Penny. 'I want him with me.'

It was as she was being carefully lifted on to the stretcher by two cheerful ambulancemen that her son came racing into the room. 'What's going on? What's the—' And then he saw his mother and his face changed. 'Oh, Lord! What's happened?'

'Are you Mrs Sterne's son?' asked one of the medics.

Adam nodded. 'I am. What's wrong with my mother?'

'I'm afraid she's broken her hip.'

'How the hell did that happen? Penny?' He whipped round to glare at her, as if it was her fault. 'You're supposed to be looking after her.'

'It was no one's fault,' said the other ambulanceman soothingly. 'These things happen.'

Adam didn't look very convinced, and continued to glare at Penny before turning back to his mother. When she was carried out to the ambulance he walked with her, holding her hand, murmuring words of comfort, and he stayed with her when the doors were closed and it was driven away.

Penny would have liked to go too, but no one had suggested it and she knew Adam wouldn't have agreed anyway.

She walked around the villa like a lost soul, continually castigating herself for not watching Lucy more closely. She'd been so het-up about Adam, about his treatment of her, about Lucy's matchmaking ideas, that she'd wanted only to end the conversation.

It was one thing, though, to blame herself, another for Adam to do it. How dared he say she wasn't doing her job properly? She was his mother's companion, for heaven's sake, not her nursemaid. His mother had caught her foot on her walking stick; it was something that could have happened to anyone.

She was tempted to take Adam's car and drive herself to the hospital. She wanted to know how bad Mrs Sterne's injuries were. But she suspected that he wouldn't approve, that he would think she was taking too much on herself, and so she swam in the pool instead, to try and calm her jangling nerves, and then went to bed.

Not to sleep, though. She simply lay on the top, fully clothed, waiting and listening for Adam to come home. When morning arrived and there was still no sign of him she phoned the hospital and they told her that Lucy had already been given a new hip.

Adam came home only briefly, to shave and change and collect nightdresses and toiletries for his mother. He was brusque and unfriendly, still apparently blaming Penny for the accident.

And when Penny asked whether she could go to see her he withered her with sharp words and angry looks. 'My mother's in no fit state to see anyone. In fact,' he said, 'I've booked you a flight home tomorrow.'

Penny gasped. How could he do such a thing? 'But I want to see your mother. I can't leave without speaking to her. And when she comes out she'll—'

'She'll be flown home to England,' he informed her. Adding with a cruelly vindictive smile, 'Your services are no longer required.'

There was nothing Penny could say. She couldn't argue, because if his mother was going home there'd be no job for her. It was a sudden end to her plans—none of which had come to fruition.

This man, whom she had vowed to destroy, had won in the end.

The days were long and endless. It was almost four weeks since Penny had left St Lucia, four weeks in which she'd searched endlessly and unsuccessfully for a new job. Her prison record went against her, and although she had lied when she applied for the job as Mrs Sterne's companion Penny couldn't do it again.

She was back to being Alexandra Brooke—except that she didn't feel like Alex any longer. She had enjoyed being Penny Brooklyn, had enjoyed her new sexy image, her new confident self, and hated going back to her old name, which she now associated with bad memories.

Surprisingly, Jon came to see her. She was watching an old movie on TV when he rang the bell, and she was a bit cross at being disturbed. 'What do you want?' she asked rudely. She hadn't forgiven him for dumping her.

'Can I come in?'

'I suppose so,' she acceded with ill grace.

She didn't offer him a drink; she didn't want him to stay. 'You really are different,' he said, and there was admiration in his eyes—something she had never seen before. 'No wonder Adam Sterne didn't recognise you; I hardly know you myself. It's an amazing transformation.'

'So?' she asked coolly.

'What made you do it? What made you get a job with Adam Sterne? It was a dangerous thing to do. Didn't you stop to think of the risks involved?'

Penny shrugged. 'It was something I had to do. You didn't tell him who I was, did you?'

'I didn't have to tell him, Alex,' he answered ruefully. 'He already knew.'

'What?' Penny felt the colour drain from her face. She went hot and then cold and she stared at Jon in horror.

'It's true,' he confirmed. 'Adam knows exactly who you are.'

'But—but he never said anything. He let me carry on as though...' But he'd quickly got rid of her when his mother had been taken into hospital. It had provided him with the perfect excuse. He'd clearly only put up with her for his mother's sake.

Had he found out before or after he'd kissed her? Before or after he'd declared that he wanted her? Her face flamed. Maybe he'd known all along and had been trying to humiliate her. None of it bore thinking about.

'How's Donna?' She changed the subject abruptly. 'Are you two married yet?'

Jon shifted uneasily. 'How did you know about us?'

'Word gets around,' she said airily.

'She's well. And, no, we're not married.'

'Why are you here?'

'I wanted to see you again, for old times' sake. We go back so long that it's a shame to let go.'

'You were the one who ended it,' she pointed out bitterly.

He grimaced unhappily. 'I think I might have been a fool.'

'You mean you accept now that I wasn't guilty? Damn you, Jon, if that's the case.' But then she saw his face and knew that he still believed she'd done it. 'I think you should go. There's nothing else for us to talk about.' And she walked him to the door.

Alone again, she went over in her mind the bombshell he had dropped. Adam knew who she was! He had known but said nothing. He'd been waiting for her to slip up. A cold shiver ran all the way down her spine.

How had he found out? Had he recognised her? He'd said he thought he knew her on the day of the interview. But he couldn't have known then or he wouldn't have given her the job. Somewhere along the line, though, he'd discovered her true identity, and the thought was going to haunt her for ever.

She'd thought about him often since arriving home. She'd thought about her love for him, that had grown unwanted inside her, that was still there, that looked like never going away.

Except that never was a long, long time. Her mother had used to say that time healed all things. She hoped it was true. This ache, this yearning in her heart, was more painful than she cared to admit.

She had thought about Lucy Sterne as well, wondering whether she was home yet, whether it would be imprudent to call and see her. Now she knew that this was something she would never dare do.

The days seemed to stretch interminably. She went out with old friends, but most of them had boyfriends or husbands and she didn't fit in, and life became one boring round of job-seeking.

She was washing up one day, after a late meagre breakfast of toast and coffee, daydreaming about Adam, remembering that kiss, the kiss that had taken her somewhere she'd never been before—and would probably never go again—when a loud peremptory knock came on the door.

When she opened it he was standing there.

She had imagined him so many times, remembered every single detail of his ruggedly handsome face, of his powerfully masculine body. But even this did not prepare her for the rush of adrenalin, the impossible heat that ravaged her body.

'You!' she managed to say, feeling stupid for that one word, but all coherent thought had fled, making it impossible to converse properly. She had thought never to see him again.

'Yes, me,' he replied tersely.

'Why are you here?' It would be magical if he said it was because he couldn't get her out of his mind, that he couldn't live without her. But of course it was nothing like that. How could it be when he knew exactly who she was?

'My mother needs you.' It was an abrupt statement, one that he seemed to have difficulty in making.

'Needs me?' Another stupid question, but his terseness, the way he was telling her without words that he didn't want to be here, had sent her initial delight crashing into her shoes.

'She needs care and attention,' he informed her. 'She needs a nurse.'

'Then get her one,' she retorted sharply.

'She wants you.'

Penny's finely shaped brows rose, and she hoped that she was hiding her pleasure at seeing him again after all this time. 'I'm not a nurse.'

'But you did some training,' he reminded her. 'You don't need full medical qualifications. Just to be there, to soothe her, to tend to her various needs, to make sure she doesn't try to do too much. I'm sure you can manage that.'

'You'd better come in,' Penny said on an ill-concealed sigh.

Seated in her tiny living room, a room that had gone suddenly claustrophobic, she looked at him coolly. 'You say your mother is asking for me?'

'That's right. She's already sacked two nurses.'

'But why me? Can't you look after her?' Except that she already knew what was in Lucy Sterne's mind. The woman had remarkable tenacity. Penny couldn't help wondering, however, what Lucy Sterne would have to say if she ever found out that Penny had been in prison. Perhaps she ought to tell her? That would undoubtedly put an end to her matchmaking.

'I have a business to run.'

'And that's more important than your mother?' she snapped.

'Of course not,' he replied impatiently. 'But it does take up a great deal of my time.'

'I don't think I want to do it,' she said. Because it would inevitably mean frequent contact with this man who was the cause of all her problems. After Jon's revelation it was clear there was no way she would ever wreak vengeance. If anything, Adam would hurt her even more than he had already.

'And I insist that you do.' His narrowed gaze was tracing the lines of her body, sending her hot and cold alternately. 'I'll pay you twice what you were getting before.'

'The money doesn't interest me,' she told him with a disdainful toss of her head.

Thick brows rose. 'Is that so?'

'Yes, it is so,' she riposted furiously, knowing what he was thinking.

'You're a strange creature. Have you found yourself another job?' Then he answered his own question. 'No, you can't have, or I suspect you wouldn't be at home now. But if you won't do it for the money, then what will you do it for?'

'Not for you,' she told him icily.

His lips tightened, but he held on to his temper with admirable control. 'Then do it for my mother. She'll be furious with me if I return home without you.'

Penny couldn't help smiling. 'You sound as though you're afraid of her.'

His lips were rueful. 'In this instance perhaps I am. She's been unbearable since her accident.'

'So you're thinking of yourself?'

'Damn you!' he growled, nostrils flaring. 'What do I have to say to make you agree?'

'You could try going down on your knees.' The thought amused her. The great Adam Sterne grovelling.

But he shook his head, as Penny had known he would. 'I told my mother she was sending me on a wild-goose chase.' He pushed himself swiftly to his feet and headed for the door.

He had turned the handle before she said softly, 'I'll do it.' She would regret it, she knew, but for his mother's sake she'd do it. *And who was she trying to kid?* His mother indeed. It was Adam she wanted to see more of, to feast her greedy eyes on; she wanted to gain more memories that would help her through the dark days ahead when her job was done and she saw Adam no more.

He didn't smile. He didn't even look pleased. Why should he? Instead he said, 'Good. I'll wait while you pack whatever you think you'll need.'

'I can't come this minute,' exclaimed Penny. 'There are things I have to do, arrangements to be made.'

'Very well. I'll call back later. How long do you need? A couple of hours?'

'I'll be ready at two,' she told him, matching the coolness in his voice. Her first leap of pleasure on seeing Adam had turned swiftly to disappointment. There would be no good memories, no time spent together. He disapproved of her entirely and she knew exactly why.

And when he came, when he picked her and her baggage up, he was still cold and distant and as unfriendly as it was possible to be. There was no hope, Penny thought, not the remotest chance of his mother's plans coming to fruition.

CHAPTER NINE

IF ADAM wasn't pleased to have her in his home then Lucy Sterne was. Her reception was in complete contrast to her son's. She welcomed Penny warmly, and immediately wanted to know why she had run away from St Lucia.

'I expected you to come and see me in hospital,' she said reprovingly.

Penny gave a wan smile, furious at Adam for putting her in this situation. If he hadn't been in the room she might have been tempted to tell Mrs Sterne that it had been his idea that she leave so suddenly.

'I thought you wouldn't be up to visitors,' she lied with an apologetic grimace. 'And as Adam told me you'd be going home to recover there seemed little point in me staying since my job was over.' Out of the corner of her eye she saw his faint nod of approval.

'Even so you could have visited me here,' reproached his mother.

'I guess I could have.'

'So why didn't you?' asked Lucy sharply.

Because your son doesn't approve of me. Because I have a criminal record. She could have said these things, but of course she didn't. 'I've been busy looking for work, Mrs Sterne.' Even to her own ears it sounded like a feeble excuse.

Lucy sniffed her disgruntlement. 'Adam didn't want to ask, you know. He said you'd have found another job by now. I'm so pleased you didn't. The nurses from the agency were hopeless; they didn't understand me one little bit.' She turned to her son. 'Adam, you can finally go to work with an easy conscience. I'll be all right now Penny's here.'

The woman leaned back in her chair with a contented smile.

And was that a pleased smile he saw on Penny's face too? Adam wanted to think he was imagining it, but he couldn't be sure. If he'd needed any proof as to how easily Penny Brooklyn had wormed her way into his mother's affections he'd only needed to listen to his parent constantly talking about her, constantly badgering him to call on her, to invite her back into their life.

He'd resisted for as long as he could, but when he'd seen that it was affecting Lucy's health, he'd finally done as she'd asked.

His heart had run amok as he'd knocked on Penny's door, because no matter how hard he'd tried over the last few weeks he'd been unable to get her out of his mind. The attraction was still there. No, dammit, the love he felt for her, the love that was slowly and surely destroying him, was still there.

It had been a painful experience discovering that he loved Penny Brooklyn. When he'd sent her back to England, when he'd known without a shadow of doubt that he would never see her again, it had hit him like a cricket ball between the eyes.

For days and days he had slept badly, unable to get her out of his mind, despite constantly reminding himself of what she'd done. And back home in England he'd been unable to concentrate at work. This had made him even more angry with himself, and consequently angry with Penny too.

And yet the instant he'd set eyes on her he had wanted to pull her into his arms and kiss her, to taste again the sweetness of her, to feel her slender body excitingly close to his, to give free rein to the emotions he'd kept so tightly bound.

Instead he'd shown anger, anger that was surface emotion only—but he'd been glad that he had when she'd been equally as standoffish. He'd actually expected her to jump at the chance of worming her way back into the Sterne household, had been extremely surprised when she hadn't.

Of course she could be playing a game—on the other hand he could have misjudged her completely. How was he ever to know?

'Adam, show Penny her room.'

He snapped back to the present as his mother's voice broke into his thoughts. He would have liked to take Penny's hand as he led her out but he didn't. He marched stiffly ahead instead.

The suite of rooms his mother occupied consisted of the comfortable sitting room they had just left, her bedroom, with adjoining bathroom, a small music room where she sometimes still played the piano—if her stiff fingers allowed it—and a writing room.

It was this room that had been turned into a bedroom for her nurse, and a cloak cupboard next to it had been made into a tiny shower room.

'I'll leave you to unpack,' he said as he placed her two holdalls at the bottom of the bed. 'If there's anything that you need, please—'

'I'm sure there won't be,' cut in Penny distantly. 'If you'd just tell me what medication your mother has to take and when.'

He nodded, and explained, and she said, 'I know you don't really want me here, Mr Sterne; I know it's only because of your mother that you're putting up with me.' Her eyes were cool and remote on his. 'I'd like to assure you that I shall look after her to the best of my ability, and that I'll also keep out of your way.'

'That won't be entirely necessary, Penny.' The sharp, cutting tones of her voice made him wince, but he didn't let her see that.

She shrugged. 'Whatever. I just wanted you to know that I'm aware of the fact that you don't want me here.'

He inclined his head. 'That's very true.' What else could he say? He dared not let her know that he loved her. It was something he had to deal with himself. It was unthinkable that he could love someone who had stolen from him. But he did, and there was nothing he could do about it.

'I'm going to the office now,' he told her stiffly. 'I'll be back around six.'

Once seated behind his desk, he asked Personnel to send up their file on Donna Jackson. He'd been meaning to take a look at it for ages, but had never seemed to find the time.

A few days ago he'd asked Jon Byrne how his relationship with her was working out.

Surprisingly, Jon hadn't looked very happy. 'It's all right, I suppose,' he admitted. 'But I want to get married at the end of the year and Donna's not keen.'

'Why's that?'

'Because she's a career woman at heart. She's afraid that if she gets married she'll be relegated to a life of domesticity and babies. She says she likes it just the way it is.'

'Are you living together?'

'No.' Jon shook his head. 'I suggested she move in with me but she doesn't want to.'

'An independent woman, eh?'

'I guess so. I can understand it to a certain extent, because she has a beautiful home. I kid her sometimes about affording it on her salary, but she says she's nothing else to spend her money on.'

Except clothes, thought Adam. She was always beautifully and expensively dressed. 'So why don't you move in with her?' It seemed a logical solution.

Jon shrugged. 'I stay the odd night, but that's all she allows.'

Not a very satisfactory arrangement, Adam decided, and he recalled their conversation now as he sifted through Donna Jackson's file.

Penny enjoyed looking after Lucy Sterne. The woman never complained, even though it irritated her that her mobility was impaired. 'The surgeon told me it will take months for my muscle control to come back, but I'm not going to let this thing beat me,' she said determinedly.

She walked around her apartment using only her walking stick, having discarded the crutches the hospital had given her, and she did her exercises thoroughly and regularly and was always cheerful.

They both had their meals in Lucy's sitting room, at a table in the bay where the spring sunshine warmed them, and the garden was a delight to look at. Sometimes Adam joined them, but Penny was happier when he remained absent. Since discovering that he knew who she was she felt uncomfortable in his presence. In fact she kept waiting for the axe to drop.

She'd been there for over a week when Lucy Sterne said crisply, 'How long are you two going to keep up this hostility?' Adam had for once dined with them, but now he'd gone, declaring he had work to catch up on. 'I could cut the tension with a knife whenever you're together.'

Penny shrugged and tried to look uncaring. 'It's not my fault.'

'So it's Adam's. Is that what you're saying?'

Penny shrugged again. 'It's one of those things.'

'What things?' asked Lucy sharply, her pale blue eyes never leaving Penny's face. 'Don't you think the pair of you ought to sit down and iron out your problems?'

'We don't have a problem,' lied Penny, her fingers twisting uneasily in her lap.

'Oh, I think you do,' said his mother. 'And if you won't tell me what it is then I shall ask Adam.'

'Mrs Sterne,' said Penny earnestly, 'I know you brought me here because of your son, and not because you really need me, but surely if Adam doesn't want to be friends then that's up to him.'

'And you don't mind?'

Penny was not quick enough hiding her feelings.

'Of course you do. You love my son, don't you? And he has to be stupid or blind not to see it.'

Penny squirmed. She ought never to underestimate this woman. 'Regardless of how I feel, Mrs Sterne, you mustn't say anything to him.'

'But he loves you; I know he does. All it needs is—'

'Mrs Sterne, you cannot possibly know how Adam feels. He doesn't love me. He wanted me at one time, he wanted my body, he wanted an affair, but when I wouldn't agree to it that was the end.'

Had he known then who she was? Or was it only since that he'd found out? Was this the reason for his cold shoulder treatment? 'He doesn't even want me here. He's only done it for you.'

The woman's lips thinned disapprovingly. 'I'm quite sure you're wrong, but if you want me to keep my mouth shut, then so be it.'

'It's why you sacked your other nurses, isn't it?' asked Penny, feeling surprisingly brave. 'You thought that if you brought me and Adam together we'd forget our differences.'

'Am I really so transparent?' asked Lucy with a wry smile. 'Call me a silly old woman, if you like, but I want my son to be happy. It's such a simple thing. Surely it's not too much to ask?'

'Isn't Adam happy?'

'Not since we came back from St Lucia,' answered Lucy with a firm shake of her head.

Penny would have liked to think it was because he was missing her, but after what Jon had said she knew it couldn't be. 'I expect he's worried about you.'

'Tosh!' exclaimed the older woman loudly. 'He knows I'm as strong as an ox. A little setback like this won't be the end of me. I'm waiting to see him married; I want grandchildren. I adore children. I'd have had more myself if some little complication hadn't set in when I had Adam. And with my age the doctor said it wouldn't be wise to have any more. It was a big disappointment.'

'I'm sorry,' said Penny.

'Don't be. I got over it a long time ago. Adam has been the joy of my life.'

The following morning Lucy announced that she wasn't feeling well and intended staying in bed.

Penny was immediately concerned. This was so unlike her. 'What's wrong?' she asked with a frown.

'I have a migraine. Just close my curtains and leave me. You can take the morning off. Isabel will bring me a drink later.'

Penny reluctantly did as she was asked. She wasn't sure that Isabel was the right person to be looking after Lucy Sterne because she was elderly herself. And even managing the house was sometimes too much for her these days. But how could she argue when Lucy was so insistent?

With a few hours to spare, Penny decided to go shopping. She needed shampoo and conditioner and it would be nice wandering around York. It seemed a lifetime since she was last there. She would go into that nice little café where they sold homemade cake and—

'Where are you going?' Adam caught up with her as she left the house.

Penny ignored her treacherous heartbeats. 'Your mother's given me the morning off. She has a migraine.' And she continued walking towards her car.

'My mother never gets migraines,' he declared firmly, falling into step beside her.

Penny's finely shaped brows drew together into an enquiring frown. 'It's what she said.'

'And you believed her?'

'Is there any reason why I shouldn't?' He made it sound as though she was being incredibly stupid.

'You tell me; you're the nurse.'

'Then go and ask her yourself,' she retorted, fiercely resenting his attitude. She was already doing him a favour. Did he have to be so perfectly horrible towards her?

'I've already spoken to my mother.'

Penny stopped beside her car. 'So what's the problem?' she asked sharply.

'I think she's up to something.'

'Oh?'

'She asked me to make sure you weren't lonely,' he confessed with apparent reluctance.

Penny felt every muscle tense. Damn Lucy and her interfering ways. 'You needn't worry about me. I'm going into York. I'll be quite happy.'

'Then I'll come with you.'

She shook her head determinedly. 'That won't be necessary.' But her heart was accelerating and every pulse made itself felt. How could she spend time in his presence without giving herself away? 'I'm sure you must have far more important things to do.' And, so saying, she turned the key in the lock.

'I do, actually,' he admitted, 'but we desperately need to talk. We need to work out some kind of strategy. For my mother's sake.'

'I don't know what you mean.' What had his mother been saying? She'd promised to keep her mouth shut.

'Oh, come on, Penny, I think you do know. My mother's well aware that you and I aren't the best of friends. It's what this headache's about; she's trying to throw us together. And I think she'll do it more and more often if we don't show a united front.'

Penny grimaced and heaved a huge, long-suffering sigh. 'So what do you propose?'

'That we call a truce.'

'We pretend in front of her, do you mean?' Raised eyebrows suggested that she didn't think much of the idea.

'More than that; she'd see through it. My mother's a very astute woman.'

Penny nodded. 'So I'd noticed.'

'We need to be friends, real friends.' He looked at her long and hard, sending further shivers of awareness down her spine. 'I won't ask anything of you that you're not prepared to give, but it would be best if we tried to forget our differences.'

Penny didn't see how they could do that. Adam would never, ever forget who she was, never forgive her, and she would find it impossible to relax knowing that he knew.

'You look reluctant.'

'I can't see it working,' she said.

'It won't be for lack of effort on my part. Come, we'll take my car.'

And surprisingly Penny thoroughly enjoyed her morning with Adam. He was excellent company. He was attentive, he was entertaining, he was everything she could ask for in a man. Except that not once did he give so much as a hint that he desired her.

Not like in St Lucia. Then his hunger had been in his eyes, in his touch, in the tone of his voice. Now he was acting like a brother. And she didn't like it, not one little bit.

It wasn't what she wanted. Every nerve-end was attuned to him, every sensitive part of her. She wanted contact. She wanted his kisses. She wanted his love. Especially his love.

As they sat in an old-fashioned café, sipping tea out of delicate china cups and nibbling carrot cake that was entirely delicious, she knew that she couldn't go on like this—not even for his mother's sake. Cold indifference she could put up with, but not this, not platonic friendship.

'You look worried?' Dark eyes rested questioningly on hers.

'I'm not sure I should have left your mother for so long,' she lied.

'You really do care about her, don't you?'

Penny looked into the probing depths of his eyes and tried hard to ignore the skittering of her senses. 'You sound surprised.' Didn't he think she was capable of such feelings? Did he think she was a cool, calculating thief with not a caring thought in her head?

'To begin with I thought you'd find it hard spending your time with an old lady. It's not as though looking after the elderly is your chosen career. But the more I see you with my mother the more I realise how attached you've become to her.'

'And is that a bad thing?'

He ignored her question. 'You're good for her too. She's not half so tetchy when you're around. I do appreciate what you're doing for her.'

Penny was both amazed and pleased by this admission, and it showed in her eyes. 'Thank you. She's a wonderful lady. I guess I miss my own mother, and it's nice to have someone to talk to.'

It was his fault her mother had died! The thought came flooding back with a vengeance, not that it was ever far from the surface. If he hadn't sacked her, if he hadn't involved the police, her mother would be alive now. Her heart hadn't withstood the shock of her beloved only daughter being sent to prison.

'Penny?' His hand reached across the table to cover hers. 'What are you thinking? You've gone deathly pale all of a sudden.'

She snatched it away. 'Nothing.'

'It doesn't look like nothing to me.'

She stared at him, hot-eyed. 'Shall we go?'

It was not until they were in the car and had left York behind that Adam said quietly, 'It's your mother, isn't it? You were thinking about her.'

Penny nodded but didn't speak. What could she say that wouldn't ruin their tentative truce?

'I guess I'm lucky that my mother's lived so long, and I shall be very sad when she goes. But these things happen, Penny. It's something we have to accept.'

'I shall never accept my mother's death,' she flung savagely. 'It was totally unnecessary.'

Adam frowned in concentration. 'I seem to remember you saying she had a heart problem?'

'That's right.'

'And something triggered a fatal heart attack?'

Penny clenched her fists, nails biting into palms. 'Do we have to talk about this?' If she wasn't careful she would tell him exactly who had caused it, and their fragile attempts at a relationship would crumble before they'd had chance to take hold. And then Lucy would be upset and it wouldn't be fair on her. She was holding her tongue for his mother's sake alone.

'I guess not, if you really don't want to,' he agreed quietly, reluctantly. 'Except that sometimes it helps to talk.'

She shook her head over and over again. 'Not in this instance. Can we change the subject?'

And so they talked about anything that came into their heads—the morning news, the weather, football, a black cat that ran across the road in front of them—and by the time they got home Penny was feeling better.

'Don't forget our united front,' he warned as they walked indoors. And to her consternation he took her hand and turned her to face him, ran a gentle finger down the side of her face.

That was all. But it was enough to kick-start her emotions, and when they entered his mother's suite there was a glow to Penny's cheeks that had most definitely not been there before.

Lucy Sterne was still in bed, but the curtains were drawn back and sunlight streamed into the pretty room with its deep rose-pink carpet and its cream flower-sprigged curtains.

Adam bent low and kissed her. 'You're better,' he said with a caring smile.

Lucy looked from Adam to Penny and gave a contented nod. 'Yes, I'm better.'

And so in the days that followed Penny and Adam played their game. She learned to relax in his company, not to snatch away when he took her hand or put his arm around her waist when they walked in the garden. She'd decided that the best thing was to enjoy this enforced period of togetherness, relish it, in fact, because it was all she would get.

Lucy smiled her pleasure whenever she saw them together, and constantly told Penny how happy she was. 'I knew you two were made for each other.'

Penny wisely said nothing.

But then the touching changed to light caresses, and kisses on her brow or cheek, and it was all Penny could do to contain her surges of desire, to hide the excitement that she felt. She wanted to tell him to stop, because she knew the fruitlessness of it, the despair she would feel afterwards, but she couldn't—because of his mother.

Always his mother.

It worried her sometimes, because the day was going to come when her job here was over, when her relationship with Adam came to an end. What would Lucy say then? How would she react? Would she find some other excuse to keep them together?

'A penny for them.'

Penny hadn't heard Adam enter his mother's sitting room. Lucy was taking her afternoon nap and Penny had a book in her lap but she wasn't reading.

Her eyes were a little startled as she looked up at him. 'They're not worth it.'

'Oh, come on, I'm sure they are. Your thoughts are always of interest to me.'

He sounded as though he really meant it, but Penny refused to believe this could ever be the case. Nevertheless she said, 'OK, I was thinking about your mother. I was wondering how she'll take it when I return home.' *And I was also thinking about you, about the love I feel which must always be kept hidden.*

'You don't have to go.'

A faint frown tugged Penny's brows. 'What do you mean? Your mother's not going to be an invalid for ever.

In fact she's doing remarkably well. Unless you're suggesting that she needs a permanent companion?'

This was definitely something she wouldn't dare contemplate. It would be agony, especially if Adam brought a girlfriend home. She wondered fleetingly about the girl he'd once said he loved, who she was, why she didn't love him in return.

'I mean this.' And he bent over her and his mouth loomed close, and she felt a rapid surge of heat and fear and delight and anticipation. She wanted to stop him but couldn't. She had dreamt about this moment for so long, so very, very long.

She didn't ask herself why he was kissing her, she simply accepted, parting her lips beneath his, feeling a great joy surge through her body. It was all and more than she remembered. It sensitised every nerve-end, went right through to the very core of her, burning her up with its intensity.

And when his hands reached out and he pulled her to her feet, when his arms imprisoned her, held her against the exciting hardness of his body, she still raised no objection. She was way, way beyond coherent thought.

'I've wanted to do this for so long,' he murmured against her mouth.

And I've wanted you to do it, she replied silently.

'But I've been afraid you'd reject me.'

'Afraid?' She couldn't hold back the word. 'You—afraid?'

He lifted his broad shoulders. 'It's not impossible for a man to feel that way. You've rejected me so often. I didn't want it to happen again.'

'So what made you so sure this time?' She felt amazingly snug and safe in his arms, and smiled as she asked the question.

'I've been reading the signals.'

Penny shot him a quick, surprised look.

'I know you weren't aware of them. But you've learned to relax with me; you haven't jumped a mile every time I touch you. In fact I've felt a responsive warmth to your skin, even seen a shine to your eyes. Tell me I haven't been imagining things.'

'Oh, Lord.' Even as she spoke Penny felt her cheeks redden, felt the warmth he was talking about. Not warmth—heat. She felt on fire. This was embarrassing. She'd been so sure that she had herself under control. And yet he was saying...

'Don't let it worry you,' he said with a faint laugh. 'But, oh, Penny, I've wanted you so much. I've had the devil's own job keeping my hands off you. Tell me I'm not making a fool of myself.'

Gentle fingers cupped her chin, compelled her to look at him. And in those eyes Penny saw the desire that had been missing for so long. But still only desire. Not love. Never love. Because how could he love someone he'd sent to jail?

This had to be revenge on his part. How could it be anything else? Exactly what he had in mind she didn't know, but for the moment she wasn't going to question it. She was going to accept whatever he offered.

'You're not being a fool,' she said quietly, and this time when she kissed him she gave her feelings free rein. She was going to take what was offered and to hell with the consequences.

'You do feel something for me?'

Penny nodded, unwilling to put it into words.

'You love me a little?'

She swallowed hard and nodded again. 'More than a little,' she whispered, so quietly that she wasn't sure whether he'd heard.

'Oh, Penny…'

His kiss deepened until she felt as though every single part of her was on fire, as though she was melting right there in his arms. It really, really was a dream come true.

'Or should I say, Alex?'

Everything stopped: every one of her pulses, her heart-beat, the clock on the wall. Everything. This was the crunch. He'd forced her to admit that she loved him—and, God help her, he was now going to paralyse her with one blow.

CHAPTER TEN

'ACTUALLY, I prefer Penny. It suits you much better.' Adam still held her, still cradled her against him, stroked her cheek with a gentle finger.

Penny said nothing, she simply waited, but she felt as though the ground had been ripped from beneath her feet. Any second now she was going to fall into a great black hole from which there would be no escape.

Surprisingly, he kissed her again, a sweet, gentle kiss, a tender, caring kiss, but she knew that it was the lull before the storm. 'You don't seem surprised that I know who are?'

'I'm not,' she answered in a voice almost inaudible.

'Jon told you?'

'Yes.' Penny was tense now, her body rigid where a few seconds ago it had been relaxed. She had relished the warmth and strength and extreme sensuality of him, and now...

'Was that why you didn't want to come and look after my mother?'

Again the one whispered word. 'Yes.'

'You were frightened of me?'

A faint nod was all she could manage. If he was going to swing the axe, why the hell didn't he get on with it?

But instead he kissed the tip of her nose. 'In my opinion that makes you incredibly brave.'

Penny frowned. 'What do you mean, brave? Isn't this all about you getting your own back? Aren't you planning to hurt me in some way?'

'Hurt you?' It was his turn to look puzzled. 'Why would I want to do that?'

'Because of who I am.'

'My love, is that what you're thinking? Don't you realise it doesn't matter any more?' As if to prove it he kissed her again, a long, tormenting kiss that turned her world upside down. 'It did worry me once, I confess, but I've come to my senses. I love you and I want to marry you, and that's all there is to it.'

Penny felt dazed, and she shook her head to try and clear it. 'I can't believe I'm hearing this. It doesn't make sense.'

'To me it does,' he told her firmly, smiling. 'Do you remember me once saying I was in love with someone but that she didn't return my love? Well, that someone was you.'

'Me?' This was incredible. 'You knew even then that you loved me?'

His smile was warm and all-consuming. 'I think I knew from the moment you came for the job as my mother's companion. And as far as I'm concerned the sooner we get married the better.'

'Oh, Adam.'

'Oh, Adam,' he mocked. 'Is that all you can say?'

'I think I must be dreaming.'

But then he kissed her again, a deeply demanding kiss this time, and she knew that it was for real. That this man, this gorgeous man whom she had feared she loved in vain, loved her too and wanted to marry her.

'So will you?'

'What?'

'Marry me, you idiot.'

She smiled happily then, and lifted her mouth once more to his. 'Yes, Adam. I'll marry you—if you're really sure?'

'Damn you, woman. Of course I am.'

'You don't mind that I have a criminal record? That it will be with me for the rest of my life?' It was something that bothered her.

He shook his head firmly. 'It doesn't matter to me one jot what happened in the past. This is now, and I love you, and I'm not going to let you go again, not ever. It was hell after you left St Lucia. You've no idea how I suffered.'

'So did I,' she confessed. 'But if you loved me why did you send me away?'

'Because at that time the criminal element still bothered me.' He looked guilty as he said it. 'Then I realised what a fool I was. What the hell did it matter what you'd done?'

Penny wondered whether perhaps she ought to tell him that she hadn't sold the design for the new product, that she really had been totally innocent. Then she decided that he wouldn't believe her any more now than he had before. Best to let sleeping dogs lie.

They kissed again, and were unaware that his mother had awoken and made her way into the room—until a well-pleased voice said, 'About time too.'

Adam said, 'Mother, I've just asked Penny to marry me.'

Penny said, 'And I've agreed.'

And Lucy said, 'Thank the Lord.' And threw her arms around both of them.

A bottle of champagne was opened, and Lucy wanted to know what had taken them so long. 'I've always known you two were suited.'

'I guess we had our problems,' said Adam. 'But they're resolved now.'

Penny sat beside him on the sofa, snuggled into the curve of his arm, unable to stop smiling. She was so happy. This had to be the most wonderful, the most incredible day of her life. She could finally forget her past bad experiences and concentrate on her future.

'So when is the big day going to be?' asked Lucy, sipping her second glass of champagne.

Adam laughed. 'Heaven's, Mother! Give us time. We've got to get engaged first. In fact I'm going to take Penny out right now and buy the ring.'

Lucy nodded approvingly. 'And we must have a party. We haven't had a party since your father's seventy-fifth birthday.'

'Mother loves parties,' Adam told Penny. 'Any excuse and she'll throw one.'

And so they drove into York and Adam bought Penny the most expensive ring in the shop. A huge square-cut diamond surrounded by exquisite emeralds which he said matched her eyes.

And in the car he slipped it on to her finger. Then he kissed her very tenderly and very sweetly. 'You're mine now for all time. I love you very, very much.'

Penny felt as though she was walking a rainbow. It had happened so quickly that it felt unreal. And yet Adam was right here beside her, telling her that he loved her. And it was clear in his eyes for her to see. There was no disputing it.

'I love you too,' she said faintly, still a little shy about admitting her feelings.

'I hope you don't want a long engagement?'

She wrinkled her nose delicately. 'It all depends on what you call long. I need a little time to get used to it.'

'You think I don't?' he asked with a teasing smile. 'It's something I never dreamt would happen. I'm still afraid that if I let you think about it for too long you'll change your mind.'

'Never.' Penny shook her head with great determination. 'Not in a million years.'

'So when, my darling, did you discover that you were in love with me?'

She lifted her shoulders in a delicate shrug. 'In St Lucia, actually, just after I'd hurt my ankle. I was hoping you loved me too, but all you ever said was that you *wanted* me. There was not one word of love. You've no idea how much that hurt.'

'I did want you—I do.' He grinned. 'It was the truth. Hell, Penny, *I do*. Let's go home now and—'

But Penny said, 'I think we should wait until we're married.'

'God, an old-fashioned girl,' he groaned. 'Didn't you ever sleep with Jon?'

'Amazingly, no.'

Adam's eyes widened. 'The man's insane. How could he keep his hands off you?' And then he laughed. 'Actually, and there's no offence meant, Penny, I didn't fancy you either in your other guise.'

Penny laughed too. 'I was pretty awful, wasn't I? I guess I wasn't bothered how I looked. I'd got my man—or so I thought,' she added wryly. 'He soon disposed of me when the going got hard.'

Adam pulled a suitably sympathetic face. 'He couldn't have loved you very much. What interests me is why you changed your appearance. What was behind it?'

With a lift of her shoulders and a wry smile Penny said, 'I lost a lot of weight in prison. I was so unhappy that half the time I refused to eat. When I came out I needed a whole wardrobe of new clothes. And so the transformation took place.'

'But the confidence, the style. They didn't teach you that there.'

Her lips twitched, and she wondered if she dared tell him, and then she thought, Why not? He's going to ask me

about it again one day, so why not get it out of the way?
'There was a reason.'

'Which was?' he prompted.

'You.'

'Me?' He looked at her as though she'd got two heads.
'What do you mean, me? Are you saying that you set your
sights on me? That this was all planned and I've fallen into
the trap?' Amazingly he didn't look unhappy about it. In
fact he was smiling.

And it was at that moment that Penny decided she
couldn't go through with it. It was too dangerous. She
didn't feel safe enough yet to tell him the whole truth. It
could ruin everything. So she nodded instead. 'You're one
hell of a gorgeous man. Just about every female member
of staff at Sterne Securities fancied you.'

'And so the plain and plump Alex Brooke became the
smart and sexy Penny Brooklyn. And she got her man.
Well, well, well.' He shook his head, as if in a daze.

'Do you know, I have never, in the whole of my life,
gone out with a woman who showed an interest in me. It's
against my principles. Half the fun is in the chasing. But
you, my devious, beautiful, darling, have done it without
me realising it. Lord, I love you.'

His kiss took her breath away, and she felt quite sure
that if they hadn't been in a public car park he would have
done more than just kiss her.

'Hell, let's go,' he groaned. 'This is no place for ravaging
my future wife.'

Back at home, his mother duly admired the ring. She
was so pleased for them, looked so happy, almost radiant
herself, that Penny was glad she'd never done anything to
hurt her, that she hadn't carried through her plan to punish
Adam as he had punished her.

After dinner, after Lucy Sterne had retired early, a time

when Penny would usually sit alone and watch TV or read a book, Adam dragged her away to the main part of the house. 'I need you,' he said urgently. 'And I don't want to risk my mother interrupting.'

A fire leapt in the hearth in the comfortable living room, despite the fact that the days were getting warmer. They were big, high rooms, and nearly always felt cool, and so Penny didn't object when he led her to a plump comfy sofa in front of the fire.

'I need you to myself,' he said, pouring two glasses of Chardonnay from a bottle already sitting in ice.

'You do?' Penny teased.

'And surely this temptress who's just got her man must feel the same?'

Penny felt the inevitable smile curve her lips. She was so wonderfully happy. Adam was forgiven everything. He'd taken the only course of action open to him. She should have understood that; she ought never to have laid the blame solely on him.

'It's bliss,' she agreed, relaxing into the curve of his arm.

'I love my mother dearly,' he admitted, 'but she does try to take over.'

Penny nodded. 'Do you know that she had you and me paired up from almost the first moment we met?'

Adam threw back his head and laughed. 'Typical. Absolutely typical. She's been matchmaking for years. But little did she know that you'd already set your sights on me. Or did you tell her?'

'Lord, no!' exclaimed Penny.

'That wasn't the way you worked, eh? You did a very good job of convincing me that you didn't like me.' He ran a light finger down her nose. 'Only occasionally did you slip up, take my kisses, actually enjoy them—oh, yes, you did—' when she gave a sign of protest '—and then gave me the cold shoulder because you thought you were giving too much away. It all makes sense now, my charming schemer.'

Penny simply smiled, took a sip of her wine, and said nothing. It felt comfortable here against him, exciting too. Her whole body was wonderfully, vitally alive, and she wanted more than anything to be kissed by him.

'I think,' he said, the palm of his hand caressing her cheek, 'that we ought to seriously consider plans for our wedding.'

'But we haven't even had our engagement party yet,' she protested.

'My mother has it all in hand. You don't mind her planning it, do you?' he asked anxiously. 'It's giving her a new lease of life.'

'I don't mind at all,' agreed Penny. 'But I draw the line at letting her plan our wedding. That is up to you and me entirely.' And she lifted her head and offered her lips. 'In fact I think we should run away to St Lucia and get married.'

'And do my mother out of her life's dream? Sorry, Penny, no can do. Much as I'd like to. But we can spend our honeymoon there, if that's what you'd like?'

'I'd love it,' she said immediately. 'It's such a beautiful, friendly island.' She could just imagine them spending long, lazy days in the sun, and long, exciting nights in bed. It would be a honeymoon to surpass all honeymoons. More so, considering the reason she'd initially gone out there.

His hand moved from her cheek to her neck, and slid with tantalising slowness to her already burgeoning breast. She wore a satin blouse and his fingers glided silkily over it, tracing the pert shape of her, touching her erect nipple, squeezing gently, causing Penny to let out a tiny gasp of pleasure.

He took her wine glass and put it on the table, and slowly and tormentingly slid buttons through buttonholes. Then he flicked the front fastening of her bra, and took her naked breast in his palm.

The pad of his thumb aroused and caressed. Her nipple was oh, so sensitive, so eager for his touch. The rest of her body was consumed by fire also, an ache in her belly made her repeatedly thrust her hips forward, and Adam groaned.

When he moved, when he laid her down and then knelt beside her so that he could take her heated nipple into his mouth, bite gently and also not so gently, shape her with his hands, look frequently into the luminous depths of her darkened eyes, her happiness knew no bounds.

Even when he nudged aside her skirt and his fingers found the moist, hot core of her she made no protest. This was heaven. This was more than that. It was paradise. She wriggled uncontrollably, and he groaned and kissed her again, and Penny knew that any second now he would want to make love to her.

She had said not until after they were married. Would he wait? Would he honour her wishes?

And amazingly, painfully—for both of them—he did so. He somehow found the will-power to heave himself to his feet and stand looking down at her, his hunger plain to see, but also his courage. 'You drive a hard bargain, woman. If I don't stop now there'll be no going back. Is it still what you want?'

Penny nodded, though she knew she was spiting herself as well. She still ached for him, was still vitally alive inside, zinging with happiness and need. Come to me, my love, her heart said; take me, make me yours. But her head ruled that this would be unwise.

If Adam was old-fashioned enough to want to do the chasing, then she was old-fashioned enough to want to wait until they were married to consummate their relationship. It would be so incredibly wonderful then. She would be so ready for him, so eager. It would make all the waiting worthwhile.

'I think our wedding day definitely needs to be sooner rather than later,' he groaned. 'My body can't stand much more of this.'

They sat apart for a little while, because they both knew where their hunger would take them. Penny wondered, as she watched the flickering flames of the fire, whether she was being too hard on him. Actually, though, the thought of waiting was tremendously exciting.

But later he came to sit by her again, and they talked long into the night—Adam telling her about some of his boyhood escapades, about holidays he'd spent both with his parents and without them. And he questioned Penny about her childhood too. 'Weren't you ever lonely? Didn't you ever wish you had siblings?'

'I used to, frequently,' she admitted. 'But then I decided that I was better off as an only child. I got all the attention, you see.'

'So you're an attention-seeker, are you?' he joked, and there was just one moment, one fraction of a second, when Penny thought he was alluding to the stolen design. Then she dismissed it. He'd already said that it didn't matter any more.

It was one o'clock before he allowed her to go to bed. They'd finished the wine ages ago, and later had nibbled digestive biscuits and drunk hot chocolate, and now she snuggled between the sheets and wished that Adam was with her.

The proof was there. Every single company Donna had worked for said the same thing. She spelt trouble. She was excellent at her job, there was no doubt about that, and they'd all been reluctant to let her go. But—she made a play for every top man in the company.

She was without a doubt a very beautiful woman, who looked as though butter wouldn't melt in her mouth, and she was obviously after a rich husband. But beneath the charming exterior was a cunning and contriving and vindictive personality.

'Because I spurned her advances,' said Ronald Falcone, managing director of a well-known marketing company, 'she fleeced the firm of several thousand pounds and laid the blame on someone else. At least we think it was Donna Jackson. We never had any proof; she was far too clever to get caught.'

Responses from other firms on her CV ran along much the same lines.

How Adam wished he had suspected Donna in the very beginning. What a cunning and clever woman she was. He remembered now when she'd first come to work for him, how she had made herself indispensable, how she had always seemed to be wherever he was.

It had been nothing blatant, and he'd had problems at the time that had kept him preoccupied, so he hadn't really noticed what she was doing, but it was obvious to him now that she had been angling for him to notice her, for him to ask her out.

Instead she'd set her sights on Jonathon Byrnes, a little thing like the fact that he was already engaged not worrying her. Jon had been flattered enough to have an affair with her, and even he hadn't realised that Donna had been instrumental in Alex's dismissal. He'd been as bad as the rest of them in thinking that Alex was guilty, never dreaming for one minute that it was Donna herself who had sold the design.

Adam groaned now at the thought of the hard time he'd given Penny, that they'd all given her. No one had listened to her pleas of innocence.

He couldn't wait to tell her what he'd found out. He would go to the police, of course. Donna couldn't be allowed to get away with it. But he wanted to tell Penny first.

He was tied up in meetings all day, and tonight was their engagement party. When he got home it was like a madhouse, with caterers and florists and musicians all charging around doing whatever they had to do.

Lucy was in her element, giving orders, and Penny was trying her hardest to keep calm. There was unfortunately no time to talk. But it would wait; there was no rush. Perhaps tonight, when it was all over, when they were alone…

He smiled to himself. They'd spent some very pleasurable evenings together during the last week. He'd kept to his word, and not forced her into anything she wasn't ready for, but dammit, it had been hard. The times he'd gone back to his own room and taken a cold shower!

He couldn't wait for the day they got married. They had already decided on the second Saturday in May—which was only a month away.

Only! He groaned as he peeled off the blue shirt he'd had on all day, unzipped his navy trousers. Could he last that long? She was driving him insane with her old-fashioned notions. Except that really he admired her for it. There was something to be said for a woman with principles.

How could he have even thought that she was guilty? Or that she was planning to fleece him and his mother yet again? He needed his head examined for even entertaining such notions. She was whiter than white, as pure as freshly fallen snow. And somehow he would make it up to her, even if it took him the rest of his life.

He stood beneath the shower and washed off the day's exhaustion. He'd had meeting after meeting, and nothing had seemed to go right. He wasn't even looking forward to their party. All he wanted was to be alone with Penny. Even thinking about her caused his body to pulse with excitement.

'Mrs Sterne, if you don't take a rest now you'll be in no fit state for the party.' Penny anxiously hovered. Lucy had been on the go nearly all day.

'Nonsense, my dear, I know my own body,' said Lucy. She never took kindly to being told what to do. But amazingly, a few minutes later, she heeded Penny's words and retired to her room for an hour's rest before the festivities began.

Penny took the opportunity to shower and get ready. She'd seen Adam only briefly when he arrived home, and she was eagerly looking forward to this, their very special evening.

She knew he wanted to show her off to his relatives and friends, and she had bought a new dress for the occasion. It was the usual little black number, long and slinky, split halfway up her thigh on one side, with stunning visual detail in the form of a brilliant beaded butterfly on both the front and the back.

Adam had chosen it. He'd said that it epitomised her transformation. She had emerged from her plump, plain chrysalis into a radiant beauty. He'd kissed her as he said this, and Penny had felt the warmth of his love. As far as she was concerned the day when they became man and wife couldn't come soon enough.

Their guests started arriving at about eight, and soon the

room that had been prepared for the party—two rooms made into one by sliding back a cunningly designed partition—was bursting at its seams. The band played and the jewel-coloured dresses of the ladies complemented the stark black and white of their partners.

Penny had no relatives, at least none close enough to invite, and only a few friends, so almost everyone was a stranger to her. There were a few people she had used to work with at Sterne Securities, but none of them recognised her, for which she was thankful, and Adam didn't bother to enlighten them.

When Donna arrived, with Jon tagging behind, she didn't recognise Penny either, merely giving her the narrow-eyed, calculating look that most women give to someone they envy. Or so it seemed to Penny.

She didn't have time to think much about it, because there were other people to meet, faces to remember. Aunts and uncles, cousins and nieces, friends of Adam's from long ago. So many people.

Adam's arm was proprietorially about her waist at all times, and even as the evening progressed he never let her go. He had the first dance after their engagement was officially announced, and then every dance after that. He allowed no one to part them and constantly whispered sweet nothings in her ear, which brought the blood to her cheeks and a hunger to be on their own.

Once or twice she caught Jon glancing in her direction. She was relieved he hadn't told Donna who she was, because she knew the sort of snide comments the other woman would make. And she knew she must be imagining it when Jon looked as though he was jealous of Adam, as though he wanted to step in and take her from him.

Surprisingly, Donna was rarely at his side. She was dancing with every available man and having the time of her life. She was vibrant, she was beautiful, and she'd also had a little too much to drink.

Penny actually felt sorry for Jon, and when Lucy beckoned Adam, and he reluctantly left her to go and see what she wanted, she took the opportunity to walk over and speak to him.

But before she had even reached his side Donna came out of nowhere. Her smile could only be described as malicious, and she caught Penny's arm in a grip so painful that Penny winced. Donna pulled her out of the room. 'There're a few things I want to say to you,' she hissed.

Afterwards Penny wondered why she had let this woman drag her away from her own party, but at the time she seemed to be given no choice.

'I know who you are,' were Donna's first words. 'There was something about you that seemed familiar—your eyes, probably—and so I asked Jon. He didn't want to tell me, but I managed to wheedle it out of him.

'What I want to know is how you managed to trap Adam Sterne?' Donna's top lip curled in a snarl like that of a wild dog sparring for a fight. 'How did you do it, you little bitch? Everyone knows he's a confirmed bachelor. There was even talk once that he was gay.'

Penny shook her head, feeling dazed by this unexpected and unprovoked attack. 'I don't know what you're talking about.'

'The hell you don't. Look at you. You're nothing like the miserable little wretch you once were. And don't tell me you didn't change so that you could get your claws into Adam Sterne because I won't believe you. How did you get him to fall in love with you?'

'I didn't do anything,' said Penny, still bemused. 'It just happened.'

'And you *just happened* to get a job looking after his

mother. Is that what you're saying? Oh, yes, Jon told me that as well. You're pitiful, do you know that? He won't marry you. You might be going through this farce of an engagement, but he won't marry you. He's not the marrying kind.'

Penny's initial shock was beginning to wear off, and she pulled herself together, straightening her back and looking Donna straight in the eye. 'And how would you know that?'

'Because, damn you, I wanted him myself. Only I was blocked at every turn. Oh, yes, he was always polite, but he never got the message, he never showed any interest. "He'll never get married," I was told. "You're wasting your time." So I had to make do with second best, and believe me, second best he really is.

'You should know that—*Alex*.' She put great emphasis on her name. 'You went out with Jon long enough. Shall I let you into a little secret? I think he's still in love with you. And shall I tell you something else? I think you'd be better off with him. Adam simply isn't your type.'

'And you think you are?' queried Penny furiously. This woman was unbelievable. If she'd made her interest in Adam clear for him to see then it was no wonder he hadn't looked at her. But to take it out on her like this was extraordinary.

Donna must have turned to Jon when she'd got nowhere with Adam, and now she was unhappy with Jon and was taking her frustration out on her instead.

'Of course I'm Adam's type—if he'd only allow himself to see it,' the woman spat, her hard blue eyes flashing furiously. 'You're nothing. You're nobody. You're a cheap criminal, you cheated him out of a small fortune, and if you don't do the honourable thing then I shall tell him exactly who you are.'

'Perhaps I already know. And perhaps I even know who really did sell that design.' Adam's voice seemed to come from nowhere. And then he stepped into view.

Every ounce of colour drained from Donna's face.

CHAPTER ELEVEN

ADAM stepped to Penny's side and slid a reassuring arm about her waist.

Donna, who had regained control remarkably quickly, tried to bluff her way out of the situation. 'You actually know who did it, Mr Sterne? And it wasn't Alex—or Penny—or whatever she's calling herself these days? That's such a relief. Do you know, I never really thought—'

'That's enough!' Adam's clipped tones cut Donna off in mid-sentence. 'You know as well as I do that you're the one who's responsible.'

'Me, Mr Sterne?' Never had there been such a look of innocence on anyone's face.

'That's right, you,' he thrust icily. 'But I have no intention of spoiling the party by discussing it now. It will wait. Come, Penny, let's rejoin our guests.'

As soon as they were out of earshot Penny said urgently, 'What on earth was all that about? Are you saying that it was Donna who sold the design?'

'This is neither the time nor the place to talk about it,' he answered, his hand firmly about her waist, guiding her through the doors, back to the throbbing rhythm of the three-piece band, back to the constant chatter and laughter of their guests.

Penny would have preferred to go somewhere quiet and talk. It was such a shock to hear that Donna was responsible. She wanted to ask Adam about it; she wanted every tiny detail. But unfortunately they were dragged into conversation by another couple, and there was no hope of private discussion.

A short time later Lucy declared that she was tired and wanted to go to bed. She had sat all evening, watching over the proceedings, but Penny had observed how tired she looked, and as she walked with her now to her room Lucy limped very badly.

'Don't tell me I've done too much,' the woman said tetchily. 'I know I have, but I wouldn't have had it any other way. I shall stay in bed tomorrow to make up for it.'

Once undressed and in her nightie, Lucy took a box off the dresser and handed it to Penny. 'I'd like you to have this.'

Penny frowned, but duly undid the clasp on the worn brown leather box. Inside was a string of pearls, so perfect, so beautiful, that they took Penny's breath away.

'My father gave them to my mother when they became engaged, with the request that she wear them on her wedding day. I wore them on my wedding day too, and I want you to do the same.'

'But it's weeks away yet,' protested Penny. 'Why are you giving them to me now?'

She felt faintly alarmed, and it must have shown in her face because Lucy said, 'It's your engagement present, my dear. Not because I don't think I'll be around. I fully intend waiting to see all of my grandchildren born.'

Penny smiled. Adam's mother was such a determined old lady. By sheer will-power she'd probably live to be a hundred. Might even see her grandchildren themselves married.

Adam came to look for her, and once again they rejoined the party. 'It won't be long before we're alone,' he promised.

Penny's eyes searched the room for Donna and Jon, but they seemed to have disappeared, and a little after midnight the first of their guests announced they were leaving. After that there was a steady stream of departures, until finally they had the house to themselves.

'A very satisfactory evening,' said Adam as they closed the door on the mess that someone else was going to clear away in the morning. 'What do you think of my family, my darling?'

'There's a lot of them. I'm sure I'll never remember them all.'

'Don't worry about it,' he said easily. 'I don't see them very often. They live too far away to be close. But they liked you. I was constantly being complimented on my choice of future wife.'

When they entered Lucy's sitting room he turned her to face him, but as he dipped his head to kiss her she pulled away.

Adam frowned and looked at her closely. 'Is something wrong?'

'Actually, yes, there is,' she said in a tight little voice. 'How long have you known that Donna was guilty and I was innocent?' The thought had been festering in her mind ever since Donna's attack.

He frowned. 'I've had an idea for some time, but it was not—'

'You knew before you proposed to me?' she cut in sharply.

'Well—yes, I guess so. But—'

'Then all that rubbish about loving me despite what I'd done was nothing more than hot air?' she fumed. 'If you hadn't found out you'd never, ever have looked at me. Isn't that the truth?'

'Of course not, my darling.' Once more he tried to take her into his arms, but yet again Penny backed away.

'Don't lie, Adam.' Her lips were curled in distaste and she could feel herself shaking in every limb. 'I should have known that you could never truly love someone who'd been in jail. The stigma would be with you for the rest of your life and you can't deny that. But once you knew I hadn't really done it, that I was the innocent party, then of course it made a difference. It—'

'Penny.' Adam gripped her upper arms, almost gave her a shake. 'Listen to me. I love you—guilty or not, I love you. How can you possibly think that—'

'But I do think,' she thrust back savagely, shaking her head, completely refusing to believe him. It was just too much of a coincidence. 'You're a successful, ambitious man—you can't afford to have your image tarnished.'

'Marrying you wouldn't tarnish my image,' he retorted harshly. 'Don't even think that.'

'I not only think it, I know it.' Her green eyes flashed fiercely; her whole body rejected him. She snatched away and backed across the room. 'The very fact that you didn't propose until you knew I was innocent proves it.'

Lord, it hurt so much to think that he hadn't allowed himself to ask her to marry him until he was sure she wasn't the guilty party.

She felt cold, chilled right through to the marrow. Her heart hung in her chest like a solid block of ice, and each drip that melted from it by the very slight warmth that kept her alive was agony.

She loved Adam so much that she would have stood by him no matter what he'd done. But it was clear he didn't feel the same unequivocal love. It was best she end things right here and now.

'I shan't need this any more.' She wrenched off the beautiful ring he'd slid on her finger such a short time ago and threw it at him. Although her actions were hasty, everything seemed to be happening in slow motion. The ring arced across the space between them. Adam reached out a hand and caught it. His face expressed disbelief. Penny turned and began to walk out of the room. All extremely slowly.

'Wait!'

His harsh command shattered her dream-like state and she spun to face him. 'What is there to wait for?' Her face was mask-like, the skin stretched across her cheekbones, all colour gone.

'You can't do this to me.' He took a step towards her, but Penny put out her hand to stop him, ignoring the pain she could see in his eyes, the tightness of his mouth.

'Oh, I can,' she said, her voice tinkling like ice into the chilled atmosphere of the room. 'And there's nothing you can do to stop me.'

'I love you, Penny. Doesn't that mean anything?'

She had no doubt that he meant it, but what was love when it had conditions? 'Not any more. The best thing you can do is find some way of telling your mother that the wedding's off.'

Lucy would be devastated, but Penny couldn't marry Adam simply to please his mother. 'And while you're at it,' she added grimly, 'you'd better find her another nurse.'

'You're leaving altogether?' There was a stunned stillness about him. Total disbelief that she could do this.

'I think it's best.'

'For whom? Not for me. We can work this thing out, Penny, I know we can.' Again he moved towards her, and again she warded him off with an outstretched hand.

'Whatever is said it will make no difference to the facts, Adam. You knew, or at least you suspected, well before you asked me to marry you, that I was innocent, and yet you had the gall to tell me that it didn't matter what I'd done. Do you think I can ever forgive you for that? Don't bother to answer because I know. It's no. A very loud, a very resounding no. Not in this lifetime. Not ever.'

As she spoke she saw his shoulders sag, a defeated air come over him. He was a man who had fought a battle and lost. She almost felt sorry for him—except that her pain was much greater than his. He would never understand, not in a million years.

'I'm going to bed now,' she said. 'And in the morning I shall leave.'

He said nothing more. He simply stood and allowed her to walk past him. It was the hardest thing Penny had ever had to do.

This wasn't happening. It could not be happening. He loved Penny; she loved him. So why was she shutting him out? He hadn't known for sure that Donna was the guilty party when he'd proposed to Penny, but it had made no difference to how he felt about her. He loved her, faults and all.

Why couldn't she accept that? Why wouldn't she let him explain? Why had this started out as the best evening of his life and ended being the worst? She was so certain that her innocence was important to him, so very sure that he wouldn't have wanted to marry her otherwise, that it stopped her from rational thinking.

Perhaps by morning she would have calmed down. Perhaps then he could talk some sense into her.

He spent a sleepless night, and went to his mother's rooms early. Lucy was awake and very agitated, calling for Penny but getting no response. And when Adam knocked on Penny's bedroom door and went in—he found it empty. Wardrobe and drawers empty too. All that was left was a pearl necklace in a brown leather case. She had gone! Left before he could talk to her. For the first time in his adult life Adam wanted to sit down and cry.

But his mother was demanding his attention. 'Where's Penny? I need her. I want—'

'Mother.' Adam touched his hand to her arm and said quietly, 'Penny's gone.'

'Gone!' In contrast, her voice was shrill and short-tempered. 'Where's she gone?'

'Home,' he answered sadly. 'She won't be coming back.'

His mother's jaw fell. 'But that can't be. Why would she go home? What's happened? Have you two argued again?'

'Not exactly,' he replied grimly.

Lucy frowned. 'What do you mean not exactly?'

'It's a long story.'

'Then you'd better sit down and tell me.'

His mother had been all for Adam rushing round to Penny's straight away and demanding that she listen. But Adam thought otherwise. Penny needed a cooling-off period, and somehow he needed to find a way of proving that he truly loved her, of convincing her that he would have still wanted to marry her no matter what the circumstances. Perhaps if he gave her a few days, a few weeks, even—perhaps a month—and then went to see her…

Meantime there was Donna to deal with.

The weeks were empty and meaningless. Penny found herself a job with a temping agency who were more interested in her qualifications than her background. It helped to a certain extent, although nothing helped during the long hours of darkness, when she lay in her bed thinking about Adam.

Occasionally she wondered whether she'd been too hasty in her condemnation of him. But then good sense would assert itself and she knew that she'd done the right thing. How could a marriage work when one partner failed to trust the other?

It was hard, though, living without him. He'd become an integral part of her life. It was almost like losing a limb. He was something that should be there, should be a part of her, but never would be again.

Whenever the doorbell rang she jumped, and her heart flew into top gear, but it was never Adam. He'd let her go so easily, so completely, that it proved beyond any shadow of doubt that his love had never been as deep as her own.

If indeed it had ever been love that he felt for her. She couldn't help recalling the occasions when he'd said he wanted her. *Want!* That was all it had ever been. A need for her body. Physical hunger. Thank God she'd made him wait for the final commitment.

Penny didn't stop to think that any man who'd been after sex alone would never have waited.

The only thing she felt guilty about was his mother. She felt that she'd let her down badly, and frequently was tempted to phone to find out how she was, but Penny knew that there'd be a third degree, and she was definitely not prepared to go through that.

It was the beginning of the fourth week when Penny felt the usual jolt of her nerves as the doorbell echoed throughout the house. She knew it wouldn't be Adam, it never was, but she still couldn't help feeling a fraction nervous.

And, no, it wasn't Adam. It was Jon. Someone else who'd hurt her, whom she'd thought was no longer a part of her life.

'Alex. How are you?' He'd shaved off his beard and looked much younger, more handsome.

'I'm OK,' she answered, knowing full well that there were give-away dark circles beneath her eyes and that she'd lost yet another stone in weight. She was far too thin now for her height, and her clothes had begun to hang on her. 'What are you doing here?'

'Do I need a reason for coming to visit you?'

'Considering how long it's been, I think you do,' she said, though she smiled to soften her words.

Jon smiled too, a faintly uneasy smile, she thought. 'Aren't you going to ask me in? Unless you're too busy— unless you're going out. Then I could—'

'No, I have time.' Penny stood back for him to enter.

She made him coffee and they sat on the sofa. 'You do know, I presume,' she said, 'that Adam and I are no longer engaged?' She guessed this was why Jon had come, even though he seemed to be having difficulty in bringing up the subject.

'I did hear a rumour.'

'So you're here to find out if it's true?'

He nodded. 'What happened?'

'I don't wish to discuss the details,' she said. 'But, yes, it's true. Who told you? Donna?'

'Donna's left,' he answered sadly. 'She's left the company and sold her house. I've had no idea where she is.'

'I see,' she said slowly, thoughtfully. This was interesting, very interesting. It undoubtedly proved the woman's guilt. Penny wondered whether Adam knew where she was. And whether Jon knew what Donna had done. 'So you're a free agent again, the same as me?' she asked, trying to keep her tone light.

Jon nodded and smiled, the first really warm smile since he'd got there.

But there was something more in his eyes. He wasn't here to find out whether her break-up with Adam was for real, but to see if there was any chance of *them* getting back together.

Not in a thousand years.

'You do know that Donna was the one who stole those designs?' she asked.

Jon nodded. 'Sort of. It's another rumour that's going round. Is it true?'

'Oh, yes, it's true all right,' said Penny bitterly.

'But why would she do such a thing?'

Penny lifted her narrow shoulders. 'You know her better than I do. You tell me.'

He looked guilty then.

'You were having an affair, weren't you, long before you

broke off our engagement?' Penny had had a long time to think about this, and all the clues had been there—except that she'd been too blind to see them.

He grimaced, and nodded. 'She's a very persuasive lady.'

'And you were so weak-willed that you couldn't tell her to get lost?'

'I was flattered.'

'As she intended you to be,' Penny retorted sharply.

'I was a fool.'

'You can say that again.'

'I still love you.'

It was what she had suspected, and yet it still came as a shock. She shook her head slowly. 'Things have changed, Jon.'

'You mean you're in love with Adam, despite everything?'

'I mean things have changed between you and me. We can't put back the clock. You dumped me when I was at my lowest ebb. I don't think I'll ever forgive you for that.'

Jon bowed his head, fingers twisting the gold signet ring his parents had given him for his twenty-first birthday. 'I hate myself for it,' he said quietly. 'And I deserve your hatred too.'

'I never thought you'd do such a thing,' she told him quietly. 'I never thought you were that type of man. I admired you, I looked up to you. I loved you—or so I thought. I guess it never was true love or it wouldn't have gone so quickly.'

'I see.'

He looked so devastated that Penny felt sorry for him. 'There's no reason why we can't be friends, though,' she said quietly.

It raised a weak, wary smile. 'I'd like that. It's more than I deserve. I need a friend right now.'

And she needed someone too. It would be good to have company, someone to take her mind off Adam Sterne.

Jon had been back in her life for about a week when Penny saw Adam. Or at least she saw his black BMW gliding past her house. Jon had just arrived. They were going to see a local amateur production of *The Sound of Music* and she'd hurried to the door to greet him because he was a few minutes late. She had her coat on, her bag in her hand, and she was laughingly accusing him of being late when she saw Adam's car.

Her heart stopped beating. The colour left her cheeks. Jon asked her what was wrong. She shook her head. 'Nothing. Let's go.'

What was Adam doing here? There was no way he could have been driving by because the road was a cul-de-sac. It hadn't been built that way, but it had been blocked off many years ago because of drivers using it as a short cut to the shops. Adam must have been coming to visit her. Instead he'd seen her with Jon.

Not that it mattered. She didn't want anything to do with him. She'd stopped loving him weeks ago. At least that was what she kept telling herself.

But nevertheless she couldn't get him out of her head. She listened to 'Do-Re-Mi' and 'Sixteen Going on Seventeen' without really hearing the words. It was when the Von Trapp children sang 'My Favourite Things' because they were missing Maria that huge soft tears filled her eyes. Like them, she needed something—or someone—to make her happy.

'Alex, what's wrong?'

She hadn't realised that Jon was watching her. 'It's nothing,' she claimed. 'This song always gets to me. Don't take any notice.'

'It looks more than that to me.'

'Honest, it's not,' she insisted. And she made herself concentrate on the rest of the show.

When Jon finally took her home she found herself looking for Adam's car. Of course it was nowhere in sight. It never would be now that he thought she was seeing Jon again.

Why it should worry her that Adam had seen them together she didn't know. Adam was the past. Jon wasn't the future, but he was the present. He was helping her get over this bad patch.

Penny still felt guilty at times about Lucy, and often she thought about ringing her to see how she was progressing. But the knowledge that Adam's mother would want a blow by blow account of what had gone wrong always stopped her.

Had Adam ever told his mother what she'd supposedly done? Did Lucy Sterne know about her wrongful imprisonment? It wouldn't have surprised her to see Lucy Sterne on her door step one day, demanding that she and Adam make it up.

But it never happened—and she never saw Adam's car again. She continued to see Jon, though not every night, and their relationship never went beyond the bounds of friendship. She realised now that that was all it ever had been—on her part anyway. She'd never loved him like she loved Adam. Still did. She was kidding herself when she said that she didn't.

Spring had almost turned into summer. May blossom scented the air, huge white candles of flowers graced the horse chestnut trees, and Penny still worked for the agency. They were busier now, with holidays coming up, and she was asked to do a three-week spell at a small new home security company that had opened in Knaresborough. It was eighteen miles away, but they offered more money, with expenses on top, and she decided she'd be a fool to turn it down.

It was a mistake. She walked into the building, and the first person she saw was Adam Sterne.

'You must be Miss Brooke from the agency?' He walked towards her, his hand outstretched. 'My lifesaver. Adam Sterne. You'll be working for me. Please, come this way.'

She said nothing in front of the girl he'd been talking to, but the second he'd ushered her into his office and closed the door she burst out. 'What game are you playing?'

'It's not a game, Penny. I'm deadly serious.'

'Serious in what way?' she demanded to know. 'About work? There are plenty of unemployed people; it doesn't have to be me. I refuse to believe that it's coincidence that's brought me here today.'

'You're right, it isn't,' he said, not looking in the least contrite. 'But I knew you'd refuse to see me any other way. Please, sit down. Coffee?'

Penny remained standing. 'No, thanks. You set this whole thing up just so that you could speak with me?'

'Guilty as accused,' he agreed. 'How serious are you and Jon?'

Straight to the point. No messing around. Perhaps as well, because she was in no mood for it. 'I don't think that's any of your business.' Her chin was high, her eyes bright and feverish. And the grey businesslike suit she wore hid the waif-like thinness of her body.

Adam had lost weight too; his face was much thinner, much gaunter and paler, as though he'd spent all his time indoors. It was probably setting up this company that had done it. He'd worked all the hours God gave to get it off the ground.

It was quite an impressive set-up. From the outside she had seen a plain, ordinary red-brick building, not new,

probably built twenty or thirty years ago, but inside everything had been ripped out and replaced.

'Elegance' was the word for it. Discreet pastels—peach
and beige and grey. Soft leather seats. Glass and steel. Light
and modern. It would be easy to relax here—if it weren't
for Adam Sterne.

'I'd like to make it my business,' he said.

She shot him a look of pure hatred. 'Ask Jon, then. I
have no desire to talk about my relationships with you.'

'I've already asked him,' he said, surprisingly. 'Like you,
he says it's none of my business. He didn't actually put it
into those words, Jon's much too sensitive, but that's what
he meant.'

'So you have your answer,' she retorted smartly. 'It's
time I went,' And she headed towards the door.

'Oh, no, Penny, you're not getting away that quickly.'
He moved to stop her. 'You and I have a lot of talking to
do.'

'About what?' she asked coolly.

'About us.'

'There is no *us*,' she protested fiercely. 'Or haven't you
got the message yet?'

'I know what you're trying to tell me.'

'So accept it,' she thrust back. 'It's over. Finished.
Ceased. Played out. There's nothing you can say that will
make me change my mind.'

'It's not true that I asked you to marry me after I'd found
out that Donna was the guilty party.'

'Really?' She lifted sceptical eyebrows. 'I'm supposed
to believe that, am I?'

He drew in a sharp, impatient breath. 'I might be some
things, Penny, but I'm not a liar.'

'You just bend the truth a little, is that it?' she sneered.

'It *is* the truth,' he vowed. 'I'll lay my hand on my
mother's Bible and swear to it if that's what you want.'

A faint doubt crept in. Could he be telling the truth? Had she convicted him unfairly? As he had once convicted her! 'If that's the case then why didn't you make it quite clear at the time,' she demanded.

'Because, my hot-headed Penny, you weren't prepared to listen.' He grimaced, as though the whole experience was still very painful. 'I was going to give you till morning to calm down, but by then you'd gone.'

Penny sniffed indelicately. 'You know where I live. You could have come after me. Instead you leave it for God knows how many weeks, then concoct this fictional job. And for all I know this isn't even your company—you could have borrowed this office from a friend simply to make it look good.'

Adam winced at the accusation in her tone. 'This is mine,' he said. 'I thought it was time to turn my attention to the private individual's security needs. But there is no job. You see, I'm a bit old-fashioned where my wife is concerned. I wouldn't want her to work.'

Penny gasped. 'Your wife! You're way off the mark. I'll never be your wife. Not in a million years.'

'You're marrying Jon?'

'No.' The moment the admission was out Penny knew he had trapped her. But it didn't matter. She wasn't going to marry Adam Sterne either.

'At least there's hope,' he said. 'Unless you've truly stopped loving me?'

Penny closed her eyes, and then wished she hadn't when his hands fell heavily on her shoulders.

'Be honest with yourself, Penny. Do you love me?'

She was afraid to look at him in case he saw what she could no longer hide. 'Were you speaking the truth when you said that you'd asked me to marry you *before* you found out about Donna?' she asked in a frightened little voice.

'Absolutely.' In contrast his voice was loud and firm. 'Lord knows how long I fought my feelings for you, but love won in the end. I thought, What the hell? I don't care if she's robbed a bank or even if she's a murderer. I love her; I want her for my very own.'

He paused, and then added quietly, 'And it's still true now, my darling. I want you by my side for evermore.'

Penny drew in a deep, shuddering breath. There was really only one answer she could give. But she didn't speak straight away. She went over and over in her mind the wonderful possibility of becoming Mrs Adam Sterne. She had clearly been wrong to mistrust him, wrong to suspect that it mattered to Adam what she'd done. True love surpassed all things.

'Have you nothing to say?'

Slowly she lifted heavy eyelids. Shyly she looked at him, 'I think I've been a fool.'

Adam groaned, and his hands slid from her shoulders to urge her hard against him, to bind her to him, to hold her as though he never wanted to let her go ever again.

'I should have known you weren't like that,' she whispered. She was even prepared to forgive him for causing her mother's premature death.

Still he said nothing. Instead he dipped his head and claimed her lips with his. Love and passion mingled, flooded, took over. Time stood still.

'Tell me, my sweet darling,' he said, after what seemed like eternity. 'Have I wasted my time and my money in generating this meeting?'

'Your money?' she queried. What had money got to do with anything?

'Why do you think I set up this little enterprise?' he asked with an expressive quirk of an eyebrow. 'I knew you were temping, and this seemed one sure-fire way of generating a meeting.'

Penny was flattered that he'd gone to such lengths, but bemused too. 'You could have come to my house just as easily.'

'And have you slam the door in my face? I couldn't risk that. I reckoned I'd got only one go at it. I had to make very sure that I didn't lose.'

Her lips twisted wryly. 'You haven't lost.'

A slow smile spread across his face. 'Does that mean what I think it means?'

She nodded, suddenly shy again.

'You'll marry me?'

'Yes,' she said faintly.

'Tomorrow?'

Her eyes widened in shock.

'It's our original date.'

'I know.'

'I cancelled nothing.'

Further deep surprise. 'You left it a bit late, Mr Sterne.'

'I'm the eternal optimist,' he claimed.

'I don't have a wedding dress.'

'You could borrow my mother's; she still has it.'

Yes, thought Penny, she'd like that, and so would his mother. It would probably be a very beautiful dress, and it should fit her perfectly with this extra weight she'd lost. 'How is she?' she asked. 'I've thought of her often. I've wanted to ring.'

'I wish you had,' he said. 'She's as cantankerous as ever. But healthwise she's doing OK. She'll be elated when she hears our good news.'

'Was she frightfully upset when I walked out?'

'Let's say the blame was laid solely in my court,' he admitted wryly. 'And if she's told me once she's told me a thousand times to come and see you and sort things out.'

'So why did it take you so long?' she wanted to know.

'Because I thought you needed time to come to terms

with things,' he explained patiently. 'And nor is it possible,' he pointed out with an ironic twist to his lips, 'to set up a new company overnight.'

'I thought you'd completely washed your hands of me.'

'Oh, Penny, darling,' he groaned, 'don't ever think that. There wasn't a moment, not a second, of every day when I wasn't thinking about you, dreaming about you. God, there have been times when I thought I was going out of my mind.'

'The same here,' admitted Penny ruefully.

'I can see you've lost weight,' he said, his face expressing his regret. 'But I can assure you that will soon be rectified. Maggie's cooking will fill those hollows in no time. You'll come back from our honeymoon like a new woman. But, tell me, exactly where does Jon fit into all of this?'

Penny smiled. 'You don't have to worry. We're only friends. It's all I would allow. How could I give him more when my heart belongs to you?'

Her answer seemed to please him. 'Donna left, you know, before I could speak to her again.'

Penny nodded. 'Yes, Jon told me.'

'I've put it in the hands of the police. I should hate anyone else to suffer as we have. That woman's poison. Didn't Jon ever guess what she was up to?'

'I don't know,' she confessed. 'He doesn't talk about it much. He's a very private person, always has been.'

They kissed again, a long, breathtaking kiss that filled Penny with so much joy that she felt as though she was soaring with the clouds.

Tomorrow she would become Mrs Adam Sterne. Tomorrow they would fly out to St Lucia. Tomorrow she would finally allow Adam the freedom of her body. Tomorrow they would become one.

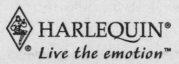